The Treyton Injections

A Novel by Stephen A. Carter

_____

Edited by Gian'a Garel

This book is a work of fiction, names, characters, places, and incidents are products of the author's story and/or are used fictitiously. Any resemblance to actual events, locales or persons, living or dead, is coincidental.

ISBN-13: 9780615803081
ISBN-10: 0615803083

To my amazing Family and friends.

*To my parents Ava and Kenneth Carter for
teaching me that anything is possible.
Every step of the way through my life
you've poured into me and now my only
wish is to keep making you proud.
To my friends who have been there for me
all the way. The ones who knew my
dreams, my ambitions, and helped me get
there.*

_____

CHAPTER ONE

I opened my eyes to find the sun peeking through the blinds. I should have taken the black curtains at Burlington's when mom offered to buy them. I put my pillow over my face, guarding my eyes from the stream of light, and laid there for a minute wondering what my brothers had been up to. I can always tell when one of them uses my wheelchair for fun when I'm asleep. It's usually parked beside my bed before I lie down yet most mornings it will end up on the opposite side of the bed from where I'd left it.

I opened the blinds so I wouldn't drift back asleep. Nice Saturday to be outside. Taylor's football training started today, and I heard him already up, tossing the ball around upstairs. The sound of Mason's alarm from the next room hadn't gone off yet so I assumed he was still asleep. That bought me a few more minutes to rest my eyes before he got up to shower, leaving me with nothing but cold water for my bath. The thought of soaking in ice cold water wasn't how I wanted to start my day, so I got up hoping not to wake him. Nothing like a hot bath, although a shower would be quicker if I was able to take those. Baths are more relaxing anyway. Just sit back and process your day. I left my towel in my room trying to hurry up and beat everybody to the bathroom so the hand towel lying on the rack would have to do.

After a decent soak and still a bit damp, I threw on some sweatpants and a t-shirt after maneuvering back into my chair, then headed downstairs to eat breakfast. Nothing but cinnamon toast crunch crumbs left in the cereal box as I emptied the rest of it into my bowl. The only other cereal left was Raisin Brand which nobody liked except mom.

The sun was extra bright today without the humidity, a perfect day. I went outside with a glass of lemonade and sat on the front porch to feel the breeze hit my face. Taylor came running out of the house along with Mason trailing behind him with a football. Mom didn't like it when they rough housed before practices or games, so she must have still been upstairs getting ready. She had to take Taylor to practice because we only had two cars and Dad was at work. Watching my two older brothers play tackle football in the front yard steamed my soul. Not quite bitterness towards them, but an uneasy feeling towards life - my life. I would have daydreams of me leaping out of my wheelchair after Taylor threw a perfect spiral spinning in the air, heading straight for the street, as I run as fast as I could, diving and catching it in mid-air as I landed on the grass saving it from a car's window getting cracked.

Taylor was three years older, Mason was one year older than me and they would play ball outside everyday while mom watched through the window while making dinner. You could smell it from outside and we always knew when it was close to dinner time. I would sit on the grass and they would toss me the ball every now and then just to include me, and the big grin on my face when they did was worth it for them. I felt like mom was more proud of them than me, but then again I was born with my condition and she seemed to blame herself for my disability. Her eyes would tell it all. She'd see me get excited and let down simultaneously whenever we got ready to go to Taylor's games.

He played football at New Crampton High school, where everyone who's anyone went to play sports. Coach Blaine Carr was the coach there and had been there for 15 years. In those years he brought home seven national championships - which came back to back after he established his name and became the best coach to play for after his first national championship in 1992. He then recruited nothing but the best high school athletes and they put on phenomenal games every year.

I was seven years old and still remember one of the best games like it was yesterday. There sitting next to my family on the bleachers while it was pouring down rain; I was bundled up in a bright yellow rain jacket that I hated. Our Golden Eagles were down by five points in the 4th quarter with 20 seconds left on the clock trying to take on the Oakland Tigers. Douglas takes the snap, sees Drew slant to the right, shakes one defender and rolls to the right. Douglas pitches the ball behind him to Jordan, Jordan launches back and sees Kevin in the end zone, fires a bullet straight through two defenders and TOUCHDOWN! THE EAGLES WIN THE GAME! I'm just glad we were down by five points and not six because our kicker was allergic to grass. Yes, grass. He was kicking for 30% that year. Coach told him to try indoor soccer the next year and it worked out well for the guy.

I find it to be a pure gift that I remember my younger years as clearly as I do. In detail from what I wore, to what I said, to what color bracelet my mother had on. Remembering things vividly from when I was five years old at least.

While I sat and reminisced, Mom pulled up in the driveway after dropping Taylor and Mason off. Mason just went to get out of the house. His sport was mainly basketball. I had a doctor's appointment so I was playing NCAA on PlayStation, killing time. Mom was a school teacher, but during the summer time she was our personal chauffer. No game or practice appointments for me, just enough doctor visits each week to keep my body healthy and my spirits up. The doctor was great I must admit. Not just a family doctor, but a close friend to my parents for as long as I can remember. They trust him with my life - literally. I had to go for check-ups every week to see the "miraculous" progress that was taking place in my legs, or not. There's the series of x-rays, weekly shots, and a physical therapy class that was mandatory. Not getting this treatment would affect my health tremendously I was told – especially the injections.

Dr. Browden had never seen anything like it before, but was very optimistic about me one day coming out of the condition.

"Your body is strong Alex, just keep on doing what you're doing, and you'll be scoring touchdowns just like your brothers one day". That's what he told me every single week, and in my mind I wanted to believe it, but to be honest I had been pushing a wheelchair as long as I can remember. So at this point, it was planted in my mind that this was irreversible, there was no miracle, and it became a part of me that I accepted. Life wasn't bad, but some days were worse than others.

Like those summer days in Sacramento, California - feeling left out and lonely because I couldn't do what the other kids were doing. I can't leave out the times I've cried theatrically, soaking my pillowcase, lying on my bed at ten o'clock at night but actually falling asleep at three in the morning, just so much on my mind. Terrified of what tomorrow may bring and the future may hold. What did the end of my book look like? I just wanted to skip right to it in hopes I wouldn't be too much of a failure. Those days didn't come too often but when they came the ones closest to me knew. As charismatic and goofy as I was all the time you would think I loved life, and I did...exceptionally, but sometimes it was a bit too much.

Waves crashing on the shore, the swishing sound of water being sucked out for the next wave to take its place, jet skis and the smell of fuel was always the feeling of the beginning of summer and the beginning of my depression stage. My parents packed a soft lunch, and took me out to the beach to relax and read a good book. Dad usually left work extra early on

Saturdays, and left his assistant Nick in charge. The feel was bittersweet watching Frisbees fly over my head and children diving to catch it crashing into the sand. Breathing in the smell of corn dogs, churros, and salt water put an atmospheric smile on my face. I treated the experience as if I would be reading that book regardless of my rickety legs.

Friends were important to me, but I didn't keep many. It was my choice. A small circle is a loyal circle. Besides my brothers, the closest friend I had was Andrew. A curly headed, lanky, easy going brother from another mother who cracks jokes every chance he gets...but was never actually funny, bless his heart. He once crept up behind me with a lizard in second grade and not knowing what or who it was, I turned around and socked him in the jaw with my little bald up fist, leaving him lying on the carpet stunned. No crying at all just stunned. The image of the sweet kid I was made out to be from day one faded before the rest of the class and Ms. Pearson who was startled.

"Alex Treyton! What in heaven's name!" she yelled. I

muttered a few words while massaging my knuckles and attempted to redeem my image.

"I, I don't...I'm sorry." I murmured.

Andrew, who'd still been lying on the ground holding his face, got up and scurried next to Ms. Pearson. He knew he wasn't innocent but when you're that young you would sell your soul not to get in trouble. Trouble was terrifying at that age. Trouble with the teacher meant writing sentences during recess, and that was the only highlight of the school day. Trouble with the teacher also leads to trouble with your parents which carries on to groundation, limited electronic devices to waste your time on, and a possible whooping if bad enough. Andrew, shifting his jaw around, stared me right in the eyes, and I stared right back with half of an apologetic look on my face.

"It's not all his fault Ms. Pearson." He reached under the desk, grabbed his lizard, and shoved it in Ms. Pearson's face as it rested in the palm of his hand. "I tried to scare him with the lizard and he just turned around scared. I don't think he meant to," he said before walking off. Darn right I didn't mean too, and he's lucky I didn't fall out of my wheelchair. Then again that was quite noble of him to say what he said. Lord knows the rest of us wouldn't miss recess for anyone. We really didn't speak too much to each other for a couple weeks after that, but the mutual respect was there.

The first day of our actual friendship started weeks later. The infamous incident with Billy Clayton, an enormous red head who had a lisp and felt like he needed to take it out on everyone that looked in his direction. He was also rather unintelligent and his reading skills - even for a second grader were horrible. We were reading 'Treasure Mountain'. Ms. Pearson had her own method of class reading and we would go in order with each of us reading four lines until the book was finished. Whenever it got to Billy everyone in the classroom just let out a huge sigh, knowing we were going to be sitting there for the next twenty-five minutes listening to him attempt to sound out every letter in the alphabet. At least the ones he knew. You can't help but to laugh and on this one particular day I let out a small chuckle, and he stopped reading immediately. The class gasped. Staring at me with his lazy eye, sweat running down the side of his face, and his feelings dismantled, he stood up and started towards me.

"Something funny besides your face Alex?" He growled at me.

Billy wasn't a normal sized second grader, he looked more like a 5th grader on steroids and with all 115lbs of anger speed walking towards me I'm sure others were debating whether or not my pants were wet. Sitting in my wheel chair wondering what possibly would he do to little ole me, and I'm sure my face showed every expression I was feeling. He went right behind me and tipped my wheelchair over, lunging me towards the edge of my desk leaving me planting myself face first onto the carpet. I kind of saw it in slow motion as I knew my head was going to make contact with the hard wood area instead. Next thing I know, Andrew stands up and throws a Crayola pack of sixty-four right at Billy's head striking him in side of his face. I saw a few students put a bookmark in their books knowing reading time was over for the day. Ms. Pearson's face as beautiful as it was wasn't a pleasant sight to see. It all happened too fast for her to even react to the situation, but she sure did duck when the yellow crayon flew out of the box and brushed past her ear. From then on out, Andrew and I were tight.

CHAPTER TWO

Sometimes I felt like I saw Andrew too much. He started to work for my dad's Deli just as a summer job. Sometimes he would feel a little too close to the family and call my dad by his first name.

"Hey Truen! How's Doreen and the boys?" he'd say like they were old college buddies or something. My dad would even get a questioning look on his face, probably wondering if he should tell him to keep it professional at the work place so his other employees won't think it was okay to do it too.

"Yea, I'm gonna need you not to call me Truen. Mr. Treyton is just fine, and Doreen and the boys are good as always thanks for asking," Dad one day told him. No doubt slipping him a fatherly wink because he did like him like a son, I think. He didn't want the others thinking he was showing favoritism to his sons best friend, however. That's the reason why everybody thought he gave him the job in the first place. Well it was. Business wasn't at its all-time high and he couldn't afford another person on the payroll but because Andrew was like family he let him work.

Dad is too generous sometimes and always wanting to help people, which sometimes leaves him in a bind, slouching in his office chair rubbing his head. I knew he was stressing on how he was going to make ends meet, but I never said anything. Later he had to let some of the staff go, leaving Andrew and two others to pick up the slack. The Faithful Trio he called them. They worked pretty dang hard. If only we could rewind a few years back to the good ole days when summer time hit and everyone would rush from the beach and swarm the deli as the sunset approached. Business was booming when he first opened and you would see Treyton Deli sandwich wrappers lying around everywhere. Whether flying in the wind on the beach or in the parking lot of a mall.

We were a little spoiled when money was flowing - mainly just taking vacation trips a few times a year, a cruise here, and a cruise there. Now money was so tight we would be lucky to drive to Arizona for a Diamondback's game. It wasn't fair to my dad. He worked so hard to get this business going and for it all to fade away so quickly, he felt as if his role of importance had shifted. As a family we never valued him more and he knew that, but his feelings of insignificance were obviously still lingering.

The business was suffering a great deal and there was talk about us moving. We ignored it. We would never leave our home. At least not until we all graduated high school. The phone in the Treyton house was always ringing constantly. No one ever answered it because it was usually telemarketers or bill collectors. That's why the rest of the family found it quite odd that dad was paying more attention to it lately; sitting next to the phone at dinner some nights, even. When it rang he would run up to check who it was on the caller ID. One day he spent three hours talking on the phone. The longest I've ever seen. Eventually we were on to him and he called a family meeting in the living room. I felt like we were the Huxtables whenever we had these meetings. He sat us down to tell us his best friend from college called wanting him to be his partner at a nutrition store that he was opening soon. The way his eyes lit up as he spoke about it intrigued me and I assumed he wasn't going to turn it down.

"Sounds like a great opportunity!" Mason said.

Mom nudged dad in the arm. "Umm, although it's a good transition, there's a little more to the story guys," dad continued telling us.

"Well, spit it out dad!" Taylor said smiling, anticipating more great news.

"Well the store isn't actually going to be here," he answered.

"Here as in Sacramento? Or..." I started before Mom cut me off. She wasn't smiling as big as the three of us.

"No son," she said "Not in California." Silence filled the room for a brief ten seconds. The smiles on all of our faces faded away quickly.

"So where then?" Taylor asked, folding his arms.

"Alabama." Dad said. My brothers were more upset about it than I was. They had more to lose, like a whole entourage of friends and popularity. After kicking the computer chair and throwing the T.V.

remote across the room, Taylor stormed out of the house.

"Get back in here and settle down!" Dad ordered only Taylor didn't listen. He had some guts, but I was still scared for his life. A good ole fashion whooping is what he wanted I guessed.

Starting fresh in a whole new place was a little scary for all of us. Mason just sat there on the couch quietly with a disgruntled look on his face twiddling his thumbs like a nervous habit. Then he got up, and walked toward his room while shaking his head. Before entering his room he banged his fist on the hallway wall to let them hear he was disappointed. He slammed his door and a few noises that sounded like books being thrown around echoed throughout the hall. I heard a couple sniffles coming from his room so I assumed he didn't want us to see him crying.

When Taylor cooled down and came back into the house, he tried to figure out a way he could stay, and pitching ideas to dad.

"I can get a second job, and get an apartment with Weston!" Weston was his best friend - a pestering, loud, football player who ate everything in our fridge when he came over.

"Dad, are you listening?" Taylor asked.

He wasn't listening, more like glued to his laptop looking for well-priced houses. Mason's door opened and he came out of his room trailing right behind Taylor telling us he was going to stay too. It wasn't happening. If anybody was going to stay it was going to be me. The family doctor we've had our entire lives was in California and I didn't have just some cold to treat. I need medical attention every single week, and my parents didn't trust anyone else but Dr. Browden.

"So now what?" I asked.

Dad said we'll figure it out, but already had his mind set on moving. Mom wasn't a fan of Alabama, but she knew the move was the best for all of us. I on the other hand didn't know what to feel. Letting life take its course was how I looked at things. Maybe it was a better move, but it was extremely hard to see that at that time. Dad was hugging mom telling her it was all going to work out for the best. She didn't like to see her kids upset. She was probably more emotional over my brother's reaction rather than the move itself. We all sat down on the couch as dad tried to explain to us the benefits of moving, but no one wanted to hear it. Taylor picked up the remote he threw earlier and turned on the T.V. in disrespect to drown out Dads 'look on the bright side' speech. Fresh Prince of Bel-Air was on and at first there was an awkward tension throughout the living room as we all sat on the couch, with Dad slouched in his lazy boy.

Mom went to the kitchen to make herself some tea to relax her for the night, and as she came back into the living room, all of us were laughing hysterically watching Will Smith's on screen drama, forgetting our own. Fights, disagreements, drama, all occur in the Treyton household from time to time, but the weirdest things always brings us closer making us forget about why we were arguing in the first place. Fresh Prince was definitely one of them. The vibe in the room had shifted to a more positive presence and everyone went to bed gracefully.

The morning we drove to Alabama didn't feel right. It didn't hit me until the last day. The life that we built in California was amazing. Good people, great friends, and a doctor that kept me hopeful and healthy. I don't expect another doctor to care for me like he did, although the needles that punctured my leg every weekend, definitely made me think otherwise...sometimes. Also knowing he was doing it for me in good faith that one day I would stand on my own two feet - literally. Walking out of the house I took a last look at the empty living room. Flashbacks of memories shared with my family and friends flooded my mind. Things will never be the same again. Mason walked out of his room sulking and it looked like he had been crying. Taylor was sitting in the grass in the backyard with a Gatorade bottle in his hand throwing it up into the air repeatedly. I went out the back door to check on him

"You okay bro?" I asked.

"Man, I don't think I'm gonna go. My whole life is here and I'm not going to go live in a barn."

I chuckled a little at the idea. "Live in a barn? I don't think mom and dad would do that to us man, they know how we are. Besides I made a deal with mom that we're going to at least live by a mall."

Taylor lays his head down on the grass looking up at the clouds, still tossing the bottle in the air. "You and your clothes. If only I can support myself here, they would probably let me stay. I have to find a way. I would come and visit every chance I got so you guys would see me but, I just can't leave. Not yet." Mom came up to the fence and signaled to us it was time to go.

"Well maybe you can come back when you're eighteen bro, but for now none of us have a choice. It's only one more year." I said.

The weather didn't add to the situation either, dark clouds passing the sky, and wind blowing. It was not a good day to travel when it's looking like its going to rain. We hopped in the car and there was nothing but complete silence as we drove away from where we called home.

The picture of a barn still set in my mind from Taylor's view of how Alabama would be. I wondered if it was really going to be like that. I kept dosing off during the drive dreaming about our house in

Alabama. In the dream I would wake up from a deep sleep after mom shouted, "we're here!" and look out the window as we were pulling into the neighborhood and only see little houses within a half a mile apart with an abundance of land to each house occupied by horses, cows, pigs, and of course chickens. I woke up for real and there were still miles to go before I'd see if it was a prophetic one or not.

I'd always wake up when dad slammed on his brakes and mom would yell, "Gosh Truen! Chill!" Yea, she said chill, and she only sounded half cool when she was upset or caught off guard. 'Oh Snap' was another one she would use. , made me feel like she was mocking us, or maybe just trying to fit in. Mason and Taylor were not light sleepers at all. They would sleep through a tornado if it hit our house. I on the other hand would wake up if I heard a door screech, or if I heard the click of a light switch. It also takes me a long time to wind down and actually fall asleep. In the car on the ride sleep mostly evaded me; meanwhile Taylor was leaned up against the window drooling onto his under armor shirt. Mason's face was mashed up against Taylor's arm not moving a muscle. I took a picture with my phone to get a laugh in when I needed one, and to show them when they woke up. Dad looked at me through the rearview mirror and smiled.

CHAPTER THREE

Arriving in Alabama was surprisingly not as bad as I had imagined, but a bit similar in some cases in that my dreams were definitely right about the little house with a lot of land, but there were some enormous houses as well. Brand new two-story brick houses surrounded by acres of land were there and of course occupied by both cows and horses. I didn't see a lot of pigs or chickens but I knew if I went to the right area I would find them in every yard. It's not my fault I think like this, I blame television. Every show makes jokes about Alabama and makes it look like a gigantic barn with nothing but Billy Bobs', and Mary Sues. I did wonder if someone was going to ask me to wrestle. It was coming sooner or later, wheelchair or not I supposed.

I picked up on a lot from the first month in our new habitat. It wasn't a bad place to live if you travel a lot, but it was definitely different from what I was used to. The weather is always all over the place, you never knew what to expect. One day it'll be bright and sunny at 75 degrees and the next day it'll storm and a tornado would destroy a city. The people were great though, at least the people I got to know. They sure do love some football and in Alabama you either go for two teams, Auburn or Alabama - and you better chose one. Football is everything to those people and the only thing above that is Jesus himself. I personally always played football games on the Nintendo pretending it was me in real life, and sometimes I really felt like I was on the field scoring those goals. My mom would have to pry me away from the TV screen in the living room some nights. I would scarf my dinner down real fast and run right back to it, and right after my mom checked to see if I was sleep around nine, I would sneak out of bed, hop into my chair quietly, put the volume on low so only I could hear and play for another two hours.

Affected by my overly suspicious imagination, I always kept looking back into the hallway to see if my mom woke up to get a glass of water. She does that often. If she did while I was sneaking a play on an imaginary field that she'd somehow understand. I never wanted anything more than to walk, run, and jump. People say it's only because I never could and we all want what we can't have, but the truth is, they don't know what they have.

Our new house was beautiful. It was bigger than the one in California. The space in my room was enormous, and tons more room in the hallway for my wheelchair. Taylor and Mason were pretty surprised themselves. Mom took us to the store to get new curtains and bed sheets. Everything was cheaper here. Enormously cheaper, and the penny pincher dad was I'm sure he was going to appreciate that. I come from a Christian background, basically raised in the church, so the first thing my parents wanted to do was look for a church home after we got settled. We drove all around the city of Presterville searching for the right one. We saw a huge church from the interstate and decided to check it out. One thing I can say about Alabama is it's not about finding a church; it's about finding *your* church. There was one on every corner. I even saw two churches almost side by side. You don't see that in California that's for sure. We pulled up to the church, walked inside and there was a short Latino man vacuuming the lobby area. He had on a grey worn out t-shirt, faded jeans that barely reached his ankles and those Reebok shoes with the Velcro that you only see old people wear. He only looked about forty but was balding almost completely in the back. All five of us stood there at the door as dad tried to get his attention, but his back was turned at that moment. Evidentially his headphones were on full blast because even dad shouting did nothing to rouse his attention.

"Sir, Excuse me sir!" He finally turned around and flinched a little after being startled by a family of five staring at him with lost eyes. He turned off the vacuum, and took his headphones out.

"Hello there, how may I help you guys?" he asked in a thick Spanish accent, smiling cheerfully.

Mom looked at dad and he stepped up. "Hey there, we are new to the area and just driving around checking out some churches. We saw this one from the interstate and decided to come check it out."

Dad took a step back and looked at us like we were

supposed to say something to add to it. He was never the nervous type, but during awkward situations that side of him came out. Usually he'll talk someone's ear off and that person will leave with more knowledge then they intended to ever get in their lifetime.

"That's great!" the now attentive man stated. "My name is Earnest, Earnest Piedra, but everybody calls me E.T."

We went down the line and introduced ourselves and of course sat in the pew for an hour as dad talked his ear off until the poor guy found a scapegoat. His wife walked in to pick him up and told him he had to hurry and close because they had to pick their son Tony up from football practice. The same sign of relief I saw on his face was the same look my brothers and I give when dad ends his daily lectures. Taylor and Mason laid there in the pew half asleep and when they heard the words, "Thanks a lot, goodbye" they popped their heads up and knew it was time to go. Whatever they talked about for that amount of time definitely set well with dad and he was sold, and the rest of us might as well like it and get used to it too because we were going to spend a lot of time there. Being active in the church was another big thing in our family.

We got home and Dr. Browden had left several messages on the answer machine and mom checked them as she washed the dishes. He had sent us a two week supply of the medicine I need for my legs after our move and wondered if we received it yet. He sounded a little worried on the answering machine and I think it's because it had already been exactly a week and a day since I had my last treatment. He was serious about it. He cared more about my health than he cared about his own, and that's why I still wasn't sure what I was going to do about my mandatory check-ups. The fact that we hadn't received them in the mail yet made Mom a little nervous. I've never gone over a week without taking it, ever.

Mom kept pacing back and forth in the kitchen, and asking me how I was feeling. I felt fine. I'm not exactly sure what the medicine actually does for my body, I just know to take it. As far as the physical therapy part, my parents already arranged a nearby doctor to help with that. I didn't understand why he couldn't give me the shot himself but I guess my parents only trusted Dr. Browden with that. The fact that from now on they will be puncturing me with these needles was a bit scary for all of us. We didn't get the medicine in the next day either, and my mother was really starting to panic. I told her I was still fine and she didn't need to worry, despite my palms getting a bit sweaty, and my body feeling warmer than usual, but I wasn't in any pain at least. I asked her why it was so important anyway and she just said what a parent always says, "It's for your own good." Boy if I got a penny for every time I heard that one.

Four soccer games on the PlayStation and two movies later it started to get late so I got ready for bed and laid there resting my eyes. My stomach was a little upset, and I'm guessing it's from the three popsicles I ate earlier. My mind began to wonder aimlessly then I drifted off into a deep sleep that was very much needed. Visions began to flood my mind. It was like my head took me on a dark journey to a fictional place that seemed quite real. A confused, abused, and frightened kid curled up in a corner in a pitch black room with what it felt to be water running towards him from the middle of the floor, reaching the end of his pants leg. Then he suddenly hears a voice - a man's voice. "Go...**Stephen** just go," in a panting way, like he had been running. I couldn't see his face in the vision or even the outline of it, it was so dark.

Sweat began to pour out of the little boy's face, dripping down to his neck. Balled up in the corner with his head resting on his knees, and arms wrapped around his legs, his head barely rises after hearing footsteps in the hallway approaching the door. The clip clop sound of high heels became stronger and louder, and as the door opens he sees a bright light causing him to squint as if the sun was right before him. As the figure walks into the room, and the bright light starts to fade, I awake.

I stood up in my bed and looked around, checking to see if I was in my room. It was like no other dream I had ever had before. It felt too real. I tried to shake it off and forget about it but the dream was still very much alive, such a weird feeling. I took my t-shirt off that was covered in sweat and threw my damp pillow case in the dirty hamper bin. I went into the kitchen to fix some tea and get a cold rag to put around my neck. It was late and impossible to sneak around in the Treyton house in the early hours without someone hearing you. With my parents being light sleepers and me - a night owl, staying up late every night was a curse I wanted to give away.

Although the goofy sense of humor and the smile on my face resembled happiness during the day, at night my mind decided to bring up everything that I should be worried about. In the evening hour my carefree self goes away. It took me quite a while to relax and not worry about things that are eventually going to take care of themselves.

CHAPTER FOUR

I woke up the next morning with a migraine and my fingers were a bit shaky. I glanced at my alarm clock and it was almost noon. My cell phone had three missed calls and a voicemail from Dr. Browden. Why didn't he just call my parents and they come wake me up I wondered. My dad usually never lets me sleep past ten during the summer when he was home so I knew he was at work. I checked the voicemail and listened to Dr. Browden checking up as usual, this time with a little bit more tremble in his voice. He told me to call him back so I did, thinking he may know why I wasn't feeling so hot. He answered the call and immediately asked about my health.

"How are you feeling today buddy? I haven't heard from you."

"Doing okay. I just have a little headache and my hands are a bit shaky," I answered. I didn't want to make him more worried than he already was.

"Oh okay...so that's it? Nothing unusual?"

"Are you okay Dr. Browden? You're acting a bit, I

don't know, unusual yourself since I left," I said jokingly.

"Very funny. I'm great, but I'm not worried about me. I need to get you the care you need because the doctors there surely don't know how to medicate you properly. That's why I'm moving to Alabama," he announced.

I paused with a huge smile on my face. "You're what?!" I yelled.

"Yep, you should be getting your two week supply today in the mail along with an exercise routine. Truen will give you your shot so take it as soon as it gets in because you're already overdue." He had to go because of another call on his other line and switched to it leaving me excited. It wasn't the same without Dr. Browden and I sure didn't feel as safe as I used to back in Sacramento.

My mom came into the room and sat on my bed. "Hey honey how are you feeling?" she asked.

"I'm okay just probably need some aspirin and a glass of water," I said, in hopes she would get it for me, and she did. Coming back from the kitchen she handed me the glass.

"Oh yeah, did you get a hold of Dr. Browden today?" she asked.

"Yes ma'am I did."

"So I'm guessing you heard the good news?"

I sat up in my bed. "Yes I did. So when is he coming?"

"He didn't say, but soon."

"Oh and Browden said we should be getting your medicine in today. So if I'm not home let me know when the mail comes." Then she kissed me on the forehead and closed my door behind her. After she left I really had no one to annoy or talk to. My brothers were already out making friends, and my dad was always with his college buddy working on business plans for the store. Mason was outside selling his share of the fireworks that dad bought us to the neighborhood kids. He does it every year. He takes his half, which he didn't have to pay for, then turns around and sells each for a bit less than what they would have to pay in a store. He cleans up every year. He does the same thing with candy. When mom takes us to the dollar store he buys an enormous bag of assorted treats. He spends at max two dollars and twenty cents for two bags. While me and Taylor are tearing through our bag of candy or whatever we bought, Mason is individually wrapping handfuls of candy in little zip-lock sandwich bags. He makes thirty to thirty-five little baggies and sells them for .50 cents each, earning an extra fifteen dollars to add to his wallet. We didn't have an allowance yet he was never without money.

Taylor was of course running a mile or two every day to get ready for sports this coming up school year. At New Crampton he knew who was good and who wasn't. We were told down here in the south that all these southern boys do is play football, so he was making sure he wasn't going to be sitting the bench all year. So that leaves me, stuck at the house with no friends, and no transportation.

It was going to be a long rest of the summer from what I can tell, just cooped up in my room. I realized with Andrew not being around now, I didn't have much of an outgoing personality. Or maybe I was just down. I wanted to go somewhere, anywhere. Just get me out of the house. Every PlayStation game had been played to its limit, and every snack had been eaten from the fridge and still I couldn't fill the time in the day to entertain myself. The longer I sat there on the couch the more tired I became. The motivation to do anything constructive was questionable. At least the friends I had back home would call to ask how everything was going and I of course told them I was great. I can never tell anyone I'm not doing fine. To me, no one wants to hear a sob story so I was good at sugar coating the truth.

The school that we registered at was right across the street from our neighborhood, so I thought I would check it out. We would pass it every day, leaving and coming home from the supermarket or running errands. There were always kids playing football in the open field right inside the fence. The school was fairly close, even if you walked, but pushing a wheelchair all that way was going to be a challenge. Half way through my arms got tired from rolling but before I knew it I ended up at the end of the block, staring up into the sun as it beamed down in my face. I was pouring sweat already. This was a bad idea, I thought. I finally crossed the street and went inside the gate. Sure enough the guys were out playing football in their Brentwood practice gear. I just sat and watched for a while. Taylor was making his third lap around the neighborhood, and I slouched down in my chair hoping he wouldn't see me. As if he wouldn't notice a random wheelchair that's holding someone who looks a lot like his brother's right in front of the school. He had his headphones on which I'm sure were blaring, but he glanced in my direction after being caught off guard by one of the guys yelling, "Touchdown sucka!" He turned his head quickly and did a double take making sure he saw that it was me. He looked both ways, and then ran across the street to meet me.

"How did you get way over here Alex?" he asked jogging in place. He looked around for Mom's car thinking she may have driven me.

"I came by myself. Trust me it wasn't that bad." But it was that bad.

"Alright man, well how long are you going to be out here?" He asked.

"I don't know, not too long because it's so hot out."

He stopped jogging in place and leaned over the fence watching the guys goof off, tossing the football back and forth.

"They any good?" He asked. From the few minutes of him watching, he drew his own conclusion. He laughs, after seeing the ball being dropped numerous times. Taylor also outweighed them by a ton. "Never mind, I guess these aren't the football raised southern boys everybody was talking about huh."

I laughed a little. "Guess not," I added.

"Hey you wanna play?" One of the guys asked, throwing the football in our direction. Taylor leaned over the fence and caught it with one hand. "Whoa, did ya'll see that?" the guy asked his pals. The others had the look of envy on their faces.

"Yeah, I'll play for a little bit. I just got through running so take it easy on me," Taylor said. He looked back at me with a smirk and a wink. The sun went under the clouds and finally gave me a small break from squinting before coming right back out. I contemplated wheeling myself in the shade under the huge oak tree, but it was across the field. I didn't have the patience or energy for that. I was ready to go home already. I watched Taylor embarrass the Brentwood guys for a little while then signaled to him that I was taking off.

"Well that's it for me today guys, I'm starving." Taylor said. He really didn't want me rolling back home by myself.

"Okay bro, that's cool. Aye, by the way - same time tomorrow if you wanna join. Oh, and I'm Robby," the guy announced.

People seemed to be really nice overall. That southern hospitality really exists.

"I'm Taylor and this is my brother Alex. I appreciate it bro, I might see you guys tomorrow," Taylor said.

I have to admit it was a little awkward watching them introduce themselves after they had already played a game of tackle football together. He took the handles on my wheelchair and pushed it down leaving me lunged back in a reclined position. Then he took off jogging across the street. With the faint wind cooling my face, needless to say the trip back was a lot better than my journey up to the school.

I eagerly checked the mail every day. News article, magazines, and... No box from Dr. Browden. Each day I looked in eager anticipation and each one met with more disappointment. But wasn't my life on the line? I wondered. Why didn't he overnight express it or something if it was so urgent? I became too weak to wonder or even to ask. He was as perplexed as we were about the missing package, so he sent yet another shipment. When it to failed to appear we began to wonder was it being deliberately not delivered, which was ridiculous because who would want my medicine but me? Who could even use it but me? I figured it was my fevered mind coming up with wild conspiracy theories about my missing medicine. Then one day, right when the dreams, the shakes and the flashes of images seemed to be at their most intense – it arrived.

"This is it!" I shouted. I rushed into the house, and opened it quickly. My face dropped. The paper that had covered the items inside was soaking wet. I removed the soggy wrappings from the box, and there lay four broken vials that use to be filled with my medicine. I panicked and called mom right away and told her the news. Dr. Browden was just as upset as the rest of us if not more. I was mainly fearful of what might happen. I had never gone that long before without it. Mom scurried home immediately.

"What do we do now?" I asked. She looked in the box to see if any was salvageable. Not a drop. "Just don't worry about it; we'll get it figured out. Browden is moving here soon, so we may have to just wait until he arrives." She says.

My heart was still racing a bit, but I didn't know why. It's not like I knew what was going to happen to me otherwise. I guess I just thought the worst, like me just randomly dropping dead in the middle of playing video games. Dramatic I know. I lay in bed unable to sleep that night thinking of all the possible things that could happen if I just stopped taking it, total paranoia. I found it weird I would get out of bed every twenty minutes and change the air to a colder temperature.

Usually I wanted to turn it off, but I'm the only cold natured person in my family, so sleeping with a hoodie on was a ritual. My hands were clammy, and my headache came right back. The symptoms from lack of medicine I presumed. As my heart raced the headache thickened. Panicking only made things worse. I took a couple deep breathes, turned the television on, and closed my eyes at an attempt to fall asleep.

As the air blew on my damp face, I took another deep breathe just as I entered a dream. Or was it a nightmare? A young boy lying in a bed in an all-white padded room rolling back and forth in his bed shouting "Don't do it!" at the top of his lungs. His face wasn't shown because of the sheet pulled up covering everything but his forehead. His hair was in disarray. He seemed distraught. The nurse came in and tried to calm him down by holding him, but it didn't work. He just raised his voice even more. Another nurse came to assist, and he just kicked and screamed. This went on for another five minutes until I awoke and sat up quickly after a startling noise coming from my window woke me. I looked down and realized I was shirtless. I had a shirt on before I went to bed, and didn't remember taking it off before I fell asleep which was weird. I assumed I was just too hot and undressed half asleep. It happens.

I got up to see what the racket was. It sounded like someone kicked over the tin garbage can we had out back, no one in sight. I shrugged. As I was turning I saw a shadow dart past quickly. The light shining on the wall from the lamp gave me the indication. I jerked my head back around, but saw nothing. Probably just a cat or a dog I figured, but it still shook me up. My body was still hot, and I wasn't going to sleep anytime soon so I just turned up the volume on my television and lay there for nearly two hours until my eye lids finally gave in.

CHAPTER FIVE

I slept through both of my alarms the next morning. I glanced at the clock to see that it was past noon. I had nowhere to be, but became light headed as I attempted rise out of bed urgently. I lay back down. Mom came in to hit my alarm clock that started to go off again.

"You still in bed sweetheart? She asked. "Are you sicker?"

I yawned big. "It was just a long night that's all." I said.

"Well it'll all be better soon; Browden is trying to speed up his move."

Dr. Browden wasn't lying when he said he was moving to Alabama because two days later he arrived with, what seemed like a lifetime of furniture, files and supplies. He must have been more worried about me than I thought. To move from a beautiful house on the beach to the likes of a barn state was definitely dedication to his job and my family. Before he'd so much as unpacked his own suitcase, he un-wrapped a fresh vial of medicine and went to work on my confused body. It didn't know if it wanted to sweat or shake, be hot or be chilled to the bone. I didn't know if some of the flashes I saw in my sleep were hallucinations or somebody's (surely not mine) memories. But after the fluids met my veins again and the stuff went to work, I started to feel like myself again... only different. Like I'd been given a glimpse of something important and that I shouldn't dismiss. But soon enough I did and life rolled back into routine of sorts.

We all helped Dr. Browden move his things in. Mason piled some of his small belongings on my lap and I just rolled it into the house. I didn't notice it before, but on the way back home I realized how close his new house, with a built in home office, was to ours. Luckily, just a ten minute drive. I liked the convenience. I got my shots regularly now, back on the Doc's schedule. The medicine working, I also seemed to have extra energy. Super hopped up on coffee, racing around the house in my wheelchair pretending to be Dom from The Fast and the Furious,

I bumped into the dining room table knocking Mom's cup of lemonade over, watching it drip down onto the carpet. I sat there stunned as mom came over and stared at the mess, looking back at me clenching her teeth together, making her jaw muscles poke out. A clear sign she was aggravated. "Sorry Mom!" I say.

"Settle down Alex, you're going to break everything in the house! Did you call Browden and tell him you were going to be late for your appointment?" I hated being late for my appointments. They come once in a blue moon but when they occur I always feel weird and my mind begins to wonder. Then things I was supposed to do that day would slip my mind, something as easy as homework. Luckily it was still summer so I wasn't worried too much, but I could tell summer was ending. The next phase of the season started to make its way in sooner than I thought as the next couple of weeks rolled by. Neighbors were already raking the leaves that had fallen from their front yard trees while the one two story house on the block right beside us looked abandoned. No one had lived there for a few months and the yard hadn't been well kept by the city. Dad was tempted to cut the lawn himself when he did ours. He griped all the time about how unpleasant it made the street look. Apparently he made some type of impact on the others in the neighborhood because Mr. Davison from two houses over asked to borrow our edger to touch up his yard. After seeing our yard, he realized it made a huge difference. He had a really nice garden in his back yard. We would see him watering his plants one by one while we were shooting hoops out back. Thankfully his house wasn't right beside ours because the basketball somehow always managed to go over the fence, usually while playing an extreme game of horse - the one game my brothers and I played since we were real young. But all games were soon coming to a halt since school was starting back up in a couple of days. I was nervous. The night before the first day of school, I couldn't sleep. I lay there on my side staring at the clock as it approached the dawn.

Waking up was hard. The alarm clock on my phone went off, blaring Michael Jackson's "Thriller." It was one of the only songs that could scare me awake when it came on out of nowhere. I pushed the snooze button and lay there for another ten minutes, but was contemplating getting up right then after smelling the pancakes and bacon Mom had cooking in the kitchen. I wiped the sleep from my eyes. Ah, the first day of school. I didn't know what to expect. I knew I wasn't going to have Andrew with me to dismiss the awkward moments so I just planned to be myself. Keep it original. Just walk in and make friends. Well, roll in and make friends anyway. Taylor was already dressed, and stormed into my room to raid my closet.

"Hey bro, let me wear these," he says as he holds up a pair of black leather European style boots I got from Journeys. They've only been worn three times.

"Naw man take the brown ones, I'm wearing those today." I said.

"Alright, cool," he says before he darts out the room.

I finally got up. Mason came running in my room as well. He doesn't ask for things he just comes in with pants and shoes on, and sees what shirt goes best with what he is wearing. The only reason he gets away with it is because he irons my clothes for me while

I'm getting ready, but only on the days he wears my clothes. Breakfast was on the table with Taylor and Mason both sitting there almost finished with their plate.

"Alex go put a shirt on. You know not to come to the table like that," Dad says.

"Well I would but my loving brothers came into my room and stole all my clothes," I answered, smiling.

Dad laughed. "You are going to get best dressed down here son. You'll probably win by a long shot because all I've seen people wearing are jeans and those confederate flag shirts with the little chickens on them." He said. I noticed it too. Dad grabbed the keys as we scraped the last bit of breakfast down our throats. The sound of keys rattling in the morning was the signal for *'let's go before you're late'*, followed by a scene of typical brother's bickering over who gets shotgun. Taylor was use to riding with his friends to school so if he was going to ride with a parent on the first day he was taking the front seat, so when we pulled up he wouldn't look as nerdy. Good plan... no. Mason laughed as he pointed out the small syrup stain on my shirt from breakfast. Not a great start to the first day.

Brentwood Christian Academy. Dad was a little skeptical when we registered.

"It doesn't seem like there is enough diversity," he commented. Boy was he right. Not a black person in sight besides me and my brothers, maybe a couple Asians. Of course we look mixed with many different things - mainly Indian. Not that we weren't use to being the minority back in Cali, even though it was very diverse there. New Crampton was basically a Hispanic school, and the three "Chocolate Treytons" made it complete. I wouldn't have had it any other way.

A new rule was posted on the door of the gymnasium at school: *"No more Dixie outfitter wear that shows a confederate flag logo. If worn you will have to go home and change. NO EXCEPTIONS."* If I knew better I would say we changed the whole school's dress code just by arriving there. That's all I ever saw any kid down here wear. Upset rednecks were the last thing I wanted to deal with. Of course I'm sure Taylor would take all the heat and no one was going to mess with him. He was more likely to become the new captain of the football team and possibly prom prince - then king - the next year. Mason laughed at the note thinking we were going to cause some type of riot.

"Well, here we go!" He said.

The gymnasium was where all students from fifth grade to seniors gathered before the bell rang to go to their classes. Not an enormous gym or school for that matter. Private schools in the south were a lot smaller than what we were used to. Fifth grade through eighth grade sat on one section of the bleachers. Ninth and up sat on the other side. When the bell rang the middle school kids split up and went to their homeroom. Each grade had its own building, which was a trailer turned into a classroom. The high school kids were all under one roof. The gym had classrooms on the second floor. No riot started yet. Just stares from every direction. No Dixie shirts in sight, except for a couple of guys who didn't get the memo.

"Now is when I need Andrew, because it's still awkward even with you guys around," I whispered to my brothers. I wasn't going to sit with the middle school kids yet, definitely not on the first day. I was going to give myself a few days before I made the transition. The bell rang. I parted ways from my brothers and headed towards the other side of the bleachers following the middle scholars. The inside of the trailers didn't look as bad as I thought it would. Almost could pass as a regular classroom setting. I sat down in the back, then folded my wheelchair and set it against the wall. This spot was convenient. I set a mental note to get to class early everyday so no one would sit there first. It looked like a reunion and I was that friend that came along that knew no one. Everyone was hugging each other, talking about their summer trips, boyfriend talk, girlfriend talk, and I just sat there and pretended to send a text message to make myself seem like I had friends. I was really playing angry birds until I was rudely interrupted.

"Hey you are the new kid right? Hi I'm Jacob." A 6'2 kid with red hair shook my hand firm enough to crack a bone in one of my fingers. No pain was shown on my face though, just an awkward smile, yet my body was screaming internally.

"Hey man, I'm Alex." I said. "You ever go mud riding?" He asked. Apparently He didn't see me in the wheelchair earlier. I looked at him strangely

"No can't say I have, I'm from California." A few kids nearby gasped, a few wide eyes. I shouldn't have said that. Every student in the classroom started to bombard me with questions asking me if I've met any celebrities. Someone interrupted as I started to speak.

"You guys are retards. Sup man I'm Todd. Sorry about them, they've never left the State unless they drive a couple hours to vacation in Destin," he says laughing. I laughed even harder as if he was joking, but I don't think he was. "Nice to meet you bro. You must be Canadian," I said confidently.

"Heck yeah bro! My accent isn't that potent so how did you guess?"

"I'm a hockey fan and…"

"Say no more," He interrupts. "We're going to get along great."

"So what brings you here?" I asked.

"My parents split, so I'm down here with my mom.

She's great though, so it's cool. Why are you here?" He asked. I thought about the way I was going to word my answer. "My dad got a new job opportunity." No need to go into detail.

Our homeroom teacher finally walked in. She was tall, at least 6'2. As the door shut behind her she stopped and stared around the room. I looked over at Todd and he just shrugs. She walked over to the board and grabbed a piece of chalk and starts to write her name.

"Mrs. Underwood. Not Mrs. Underwear, not Mrs. Underworld... just Mrs. Underwood," she states. "I've heard it all; it's not new or funny. Call me what you want in your own time, but not in my classroom." Well she cleared that up. Looks like we're off to a good start. "I see some different faces." She adds. "Well, before we begin anything let's go around the room and introduce ourselves shall we?"

It started at the front of the room. Everyone stated their names then said a few facts about themselves. Where they were from, what do they like to do for fun, things of that nature. It got to me after it worked its way to the back.

"Hi, I'm Alex Treyton, I moved here from California. For fun... I like to go to football games and soccer games with friends," I said timidly. That is the only thing that came to mind at the time, which was true, but not good enough in my opinion.

"Well, you definitely can't play any of em" someone said under their breath. A few kids giggled quietly. I ignored it, still looking right at Mrs. Underwood. I tried to keep the fake smile I was holding since class started.

"You have something you want to share with the class Trent?" she says. Trent was a big boy. To be as young as we were, I didn't see how someone's teeth could look so disgusting. He'd probably been 'dipping', as in tobacco, since he was nine years old.

"Actually yes, I have a question."

"Well go ahead, but be careful what you say," Mrs. Underwood warned.

"Just wondering why none of us can wear our Dixie shirts after we've been wearing them for years now? Someone different comes in and they just change up

the rules just like that... not saying any names..."
Trent says, not even making eye contact my way but
has the nerve to call me out in front of the class -
subtly. A few others nod their heads in agreement.
Truth was, I could care less about the stupid shirts
and I didn't even know what they meant. The first
time I ever saw one was the day we moved there. I
had enough problems to worry about outside that
place. If the school was going to make a big deal
about it, then I was going to make it right somehow.

"Just obey the rules they are set for a reason. I don't
want to hear anything further on the matter, got it!?"
Mrs. Underwood says sternly.

CHAPTER SIX

It's like some things you just see coming. I've never really known what it was like to be popular, just more adored by my close friends that I don't get to see anymore. I honestly didn't expect anything different and most of the time I prefer it just so I can feel sorry for myself. I would always make up a story line in my head before I go to sleep. I'd just lie there in bed picturing myself in love with a girl, doing everything in my power to win her over, but in the end I always envision her turning me down. This was no different. They can heckle me and say whatever they want about me, I like being the underdog. Plus I figured out a way to keep the peace and at least make my school experience pleasant. I rode with Todd to his house after school. My parents usually would never let me go off with other parents they didn't know, but they were excited that I met a new friend.

"So what was the awesome idea you said you had to tell me earlier?" Todd asked. I looked at him and smiled.

"Tell me where they get those shirts at." I said.

"Huh? What shirts?" he asked confused. Seconds later it finally dawned on him what shirt I was talking about, and his eyes grew big. "You wouldn't!"

"How much do you want to bet?" I didn't see the harm in it. Confederate shirts didn't offend me one way or the other. So if I showed up to school wearing one, it would show the staff, and students that I was okay with it. Which would also get my brothers off the hook, if by chance they were having some sort of social crisis which I know isn't the case. Then everyone can wear their shirts again and everyone is happy. After I explained this to him, he thought it was a great idea, more funnily than anything. He didn't own a shirt himself but Kevin Massey from math class had a few. It was perfect because he is the same size as me, and a good friend of Todd's, so I knew he wouldn't mind if we borrowed one for a day.

Trent's mom drove us over to Kevin's house to get it. She thought we were picking up a few video games that Todd claimed he left over there, and Mrs. Martha didn't like him losing expensive things that she had paid for. Turns out Kevin lives pretty close to me and right next door to Dr. Browden. He was outside watering his plants when we pulled up. I waved through the window.

"Hey son how was school?" he asked. "Wasn't the worst experience of my life...I don't think." I said with a smirk. "That bad huh, do I need to come up there and box some heads in?" He said banging his fist into the palm of his hand. I laughed.

"I don't think that's going to be necessary, nobody messes with me when Todd's around." I said jokingly. Todd is a little guy so if anything we would both get hurt. I introduced Todd and Mrs. Martha to Dr. Browden and Kevin walked outside to meet us. "What's up Bros!" he yells throwing his hands in the air. Someone's been watching too much BET it seems like. We went into his house to discuss the plan. My mom usually drops us off at school about fifteen minutes before the bell rings. I have to make sure everyone sees me with the shirt on, so I have to come in a few minutes early to make sure everyone is there seated on the bleachers.

"You can hide in the locker room! We'll keep you company, we only have to wait about ten minutes." Kevin said.

"So I guess that's the plan, quick and simple." I added. We had to go before Todd's mom started to beep the horn. I looked out the window to see Dr. Browden and her laughing and chatting it up on the patio. He also had barbecue cooking on his grill in his backyard. We all caught a whiff as the soft wind carried the smoke to the front of the house. "That smells so good!" Todd said.

"Yes it does. Well let's not waste anymore of this nice man's precious time." Mrs. Martha said fumbling with her keys.

"The boys can stay if they'd like. I have plenty of ribs in there and they can probably help this old man unpack the rest of my things too. I can drop them by the house before it gets dark." Dr. Browden said. Ribs for labor, why not? Todd and I looked at each other in agreement.

"I guess that would be alright." Mrs. Martha kisses Todd on the forehead and leaves.

His house was actually coming together pretty nicely. Todd and I decided to help Dr. Browden unpack the rest of his belongings before we ate, although the smell was making me lazy. So many little boxes just sitting in his office room, I didn't know where to start. He was so organized, I'll give him that. Every box had a label on it. Kitchen supplies, bathroom supplies, tools, etc. I rolled around putting things in its proper place. He was getting old and appreciated that he only had to focus on one room. "What's this box labeled **S.C.?**"I asked, opening the lid to the box.

"Oh, I'll take care of that one." He said, walking over to grab it. "It's just medical files, that's all." He said, placing the box on top of the shelf. "So you looking forward to this school year?"

I never really liked school. There's waking up early, pressure of fitting in, long hours of boredom, homework, rejection, stress of keeping your grades up, and not to mention nasty lunch food. I can go on but those are the bullet points. "Not really...I just... I'll just have to get use to everything I guess." I said. I liked going to him for advice and just to talk. Back in

Cali, we'd sit in his office and talk for hours, just about life. He had no one else to talk to, and I was a good listener. After his wife passed away three years before from alcoholism, his son Grant went off to college and he hasn't seen him since the funeral. Grant blamed him for her death claiming she began drinking heavily after he started to get really intense with his work, staying long hours in his lab obsessing over a cure for something he still hasn't told anyone about. They thought he'd gone mad. He would disappear and take spontaneous trips for weeks at a time. When he was home, they fought constantly. She would come over to our house and cry in my mother's arms some nights and my brothers and I could hear the weeping and counseling through the thin walls. Yet he's treated me like I was his own, and Grant hated me for it.

I couldn't sleep at all when I got into bed later that night; I just tossed and turned thinking. Thinking about Mrs. Browden, and Grant, also thinking about what everybody was going to say the next day at school - about my shirt - gave me butterflies. I finally dozed off and managed to get a few hours of sleep in, and to my surprise I woke up pretty rejuvenated. I was eager to get to school. I looked in the mirror after getting dressed. I looked just like an Alabama native. Thank God this was only for one day. There was no way you could make those shirts fashionable in any way. I went downstairs and dad just shook his head grinning.

"Going to change the whole epidemic are we?" he said jokingly. "Saving the world, one private school at a time" I followed.

"Well just make sure you don't cause any trouble superman." he said. I grabbed a piece of toast off Dad's plate as we both walked out the house. Mom wasn't feeling well and the other two went to school with their friends, of course.

"I can't promise anything. Where there's a hero there's a villain. So if I get suspended, you can't be mad" I said with a smirk. Dad laughed as he put my wheelchair in the back seat. "You watch too many movies." he said.

On the way to school I had that nervous feeling in the

pit of my stomach and my hands were shaking extremely fast like I just drank an entire pot of coffee. "Alright son, show them how we roll!" Dad says, trying to be cool as usual. I got out of the car and rolled towards the door of the gymnasium, with butterflies still in my stomach anticipating what was going to happen next. How were people going to react? It was five minutes until the bell rang and the parking lot was full so I knew the entire middle and high school were on the bleachers already. I guess the locker room plan was out. As I started to go in, Todd ran up to the door after his mom dropped him off.

"You didn't think I was going to let you go in alone did you?" He said. We did our corny handshake we made up to impress some girls (hasn't quite worked yet).

"Let's do this!" I said as we enter the gym to see the entire bleachers covered with students. As the door shuts behind me, everyone turns and looks our way. Gasps echoed throughout the place and then it was silent for a few seconds, followed by an outburst of laughter filling the room. One guy stood up and yelled

"Yeeeaaaaaaaawhhoooooo!" Todd and I looked at each other like we were cool. We were cool. I rolled to a cleared space towards the middle row of bleachers; slapping hands with everyone I passed. Trent even gave me a nod. My brothers just sat there and laughed. It was a proud moment for them even if they didn't want to admit it. Most of the students in homeroom couldn't even focus on the lesson. My shirt was obviously a distraction and the main focal point of everyone's entertainment. There was giggling nonstop the entire period and Mrs. Carson wasn't pleased.

"Mr. Treyton can I speak to you for a quick second outside please?" The class simmered down, only peppered by a few 'uh oh' sounds from the nosey ones. "Sure!" I said confidently, as if I wasn't scared at all. I actually wasn't scared, and that made me seem a little bit cooler in my perspective. I've never done anything remotely disrespectful in a school setting so I saw myself as a rule breaking outlaw.

"What is the point of this Mr. Treyton?" She asked.

"Well, I just thought since they can't wear their shirts anymore because of me I thought I'd make it right."

She put her hand on my shoulder and smiled. "That's sweet of you, but it's more to it than just you and your brothers coming here."

I thought about it for a second and didn't see any other reason. Then an announcement came over the intercom. "Alex Treyton please come to the principal's office." I heard laughter from almost every classroom through the walls. Mrs. Carson shrugs. This was probably the most entertainment that place had ever seen besides a well-known country singer coming to town for a concert. "Go ahead and see what he wants Alex and hurry back to class," She said.

I wasn't nervous at all. What could I possibly get in trouble for? Anyone else wearing the Dixie outfitter should probably worry about getting some type of punishment, but me? Not a chance. I made my way to his office and knocked on the door. He didn't answer right away. The door had a window covered with blinds and I took a peak through a little opening in the blinds to find him clipping his toe nails. I knocked again except a little harder this time. "Keep your shirt on out there! I'll be with you in a second!"

Principal Covlen wasn't such a nice guy. Or so I've heard. Todd told me he expelled a kid last year for stopping up the toilet after having diarrhea and flooding the entire bathroom. It was an accident of course. It leaked all the way to the lobby and ruined the carpet. Apparently it cost a pretty penny to get everything fixed and back to normal. That couldn't happen to me, I don't like sitting on public toilets anyhow.

"Come on in son." He says. I open the door gently and wheeled over to the front of his desk. "You wanted to see me sir?"

His office was impressive, and very spacious. I take it just from looking around, the man likes golf. Everything in his office had something to do with golf, as well as many autographed pictures on his wall from well know golfers. Not to forget the mini golf set up he had in the corner. I'm sure that's what he did all day if he's not being taken away by unruly kids and new guys in Dixie outfitter wear.

"Yes...yes. what umm... what is the meaning of all of this?" He asked as he reaches over and tugs at my shirt. I flinched a little being caught off guard. "I don't have a problem with the shirts Mr. Covlen. Neither do my brothers." I said.

"What do you mean Alex?" He asked. He took a sip of his coffee and stares me in the eyes. So I stare right back. "In first period the other day I was getting heckled by some of the students saying we're the reason they can't wear their shirts. I don't even know what the shirts mean so I ...we, can care less." I say.

"Not everything is about you Alex. The sooner you realize that the better."

"But...why would you just--" he interrupts me. "We thought about doing this for a few years now. It was just bad timing for you and your brothers, and you ended up looking like the cause of the situation." He says.

"I don't want to be the cause or look like it. I'm in a new school and things are hard enough trying to fit in as you can imagine." I said sternly looking down at my legs. Whoa. I didn't know I had that in me. I felt myself breathing a little heavier after I paused. Mr. Covlen took another sip of his coffee then got up out of his desk. He walks over to his mini golf set up in the corner. "I can understand that kid." He says. He hits the ball in the hole. "I tell you what. Chapel is tomorrow and I'll address the reason behind it all then. That way you won't be looked at as the cause of it all... how's that?" He says. "Fine. I suppose...um... thank you sir." I say.

"You can go back to class now son," He says. "Just wear this shirt instead." He hands me a golf polo shirt that was a little big on me, but looked pretty expensive. "Thanks again" I add. I head back to class and everyone is still giggling when I come in the door. I can tell everyone was eager to know what happened, especially Todd and Kevin.

I was going to fill them in at lunch time but my unexpected day of mass attention ended early when mom checked me out after she got word Dr. Browden collapsed in his garden and was taken to the hospital by Kevin's mother. As always Taylor and Mason always had their own rides home. Mom drove faster than I'd ever seen her drive before, running red lights and strapping her seatbelt on almost ten minutes after we had taken off. I hoped he was ok. He was sure enough part of our family and if anything happened to him it would feel the same as losing a family member.

CHAPTER SEVEN

Mom wasted no time trying to find parking. She pulled up in the front at the round about that read 'NO PARKING Unload Only' and parked anyway. I didn't expect our car to be there when we got back but if she was ok with it then so was I. As we went inside, the secretary was at least helpful and immediately led us to his room. I was at the hospital frequently so all of the nurses knew our family. I could tell this felt like the longest elevator ride ever to mom. She was anxious and couldn't stand still. I don't know why I was so calm. Everything happened so fast and I kind of felt bad that the events from earlier were still lingering in my mind. The nurse opened the door to the room and we saw him lying there resting.

"Should we wake him mom?" I asked. He looked sound asleep but even I can wake up to a light noise. Mom looked at the nurse for permission. "He's stable now so it should be okay. Just be quiet." She says. He looked so peaceful I didn't want to wake him. Mom just stood by his bedside. Dad would have made it but he was three hours away on business and my brothers still didn't know yet. I went next to Mom and grabbed his hand gently. After holding it for a couple minutes I felt a slight grip. His eyes began to open and he tried to smile, but only got one side of his grin up.

"Hey kiddo." He whispers. "I'm a silly old man trying to hang my..."

"Shhh don't talk." Mom interrupted. "You can tell us everything when you are well rested okay."

"I just need to tell you something about Ale..."

Mom interrupts again, "You don't have to be a doctor right now. We are fine, and we are here for you now."

The doctor comes in with his clipboard. "Hi folks I'm Dr. Murphy. Looks like doctors need doctors too huh?" He says chuckling a little. I take it Dr. Browden was going to be okay by how jolly Murphy came in the door.

"Hi, I'm Doreen. So everything is okay right? What happened?" Mom asked.

"Yes darlin he's gonna be fine. We found some unfamiliar chemicals in his blood stream and they're running test right now, but whatever it is, it made his muscles weak, and he passed out while hanging flowers in his backyard. He broke his arm and suffered a mild concussion, but he'll be fine." He says. Mom looked puzzled.

"Chemicals? From what?" She asked.

"Like I said, we are unfamiliar with this chemical or whatever was in his system, but we took some blood samples and we'll know more soon enough."

Browden stayed overnight to rest and mom was going to pick him up the next afternoon. As for me, I checked my phone and I had 13 text messages since I'd left the school. I thought I became popular within hours until I saw eight of them were from Todd, one from Kevin, and the others from Mason. Not one girl.

I didn't start to like school until I hit 9th grade. I felt at home for once like I was in a place where everyone knew me and I didn't have to worry about people judging me. That was always my problem, always worrying about what people thought about me. If it was that easy to take away, trust me I would have done it. Now, I was kind of cool for once, or at least everybody knew me. It was the beginning of the school at Brentwood and the first day of school was always the best. The reason behind that is we always had a foreign exchange student every year, and to our luck it was always a girl. A beautiful girl - that knew nothing about any of us and our crazy reputations; so it gave us a fresh start to make a new impression on someone. I, on the other hand, knew I had no shot. Todd would always tease me when a gorgeous girl came around. "Watch her end up liking Treyton, girls love a guy with hot wheels haha!" And he would be the only one laughing. Mostly because the people around didn't know I was cool with wheelchair jokes, as long as it's all in fun. Then again he just wasn't funny that begin with.

Todd started coming to the doctor with me in hopes that I would get some good news. He would listen in on what Dr. Browden would say and ask question after question like it was him that was in the wheelchair. That showed me he genuinely did care, and the one true friend I grew to count on. He also had random check-ups at the same hospital. You name it he was allergic to it, and so we would pick him up from his house on the way there. Peanuts, oysters, lotions with fragrance, he was always breaking out because he got a hold of something that did not react well with his body.

The day after my wardrobe malfunction I rolled into class and to my surprise my usual seat was taken, by the most beautiful girl I had ever seen. Dark hair, tan, green eyes, beautiful smile, and a cute little mole right above her chin, on the left. Mrs. Halloway, our History teacher, introduced her to the class.

"Class this is Venessa Boswell, she is our new student from Arizona." I paused at the door taking it all in while my Mrs. Halloway thought she would amuse the class by pointing out I was in love just by seeing my eyes widen big when I saw her. "Alright there Mr. Treyton, she's single so we'll match you two up later, but for now its history time."

Really Mrs. Halloway? Really? You can tell I was embarrassed by the blank look in my face, not to mention me bumping in to every desk on the way to another desk since new girl had taken mine. I got to sit next to 'Sneezing Cedrick'. I swear this kid carried the cold with him year round, and I was bound to get it next. I went home that day and I couldn't get her out of my mind. I mean I had never been in a relationship before, but if I was, I imagine that would be the type of girl I would want.

I fell asleep late that night dreaming only of what could be and woke up to a loud noise of "BEEP... BEEP... BEEP....BEEP" and fell out of my bed pulling my covers down with me. "FREAK!" That was my favorite word to say when I was temporarily frustrated. Crawling up to my window ledge, I looked outside the window and a family was moving in next door, and a huge truck was backing into their driveway. "You up Alex!?" My mom was my alarm clock, but the only problem was she would come on after I had already wakened up to the sound of 'Thriller'.

"Yes mom, I'm up!" As always. Waking up in the Treyton house was like waking up to the smell of Christmas. Pancakes and eggs for breakfast, and cinnamon rolls were in the oven just seconds from coming out. We loved taking those for part of our lunch. I got dressed for school and had a pretty normal day up until 5th period. We had a little science quiz but it was open book. That was Mrs. Harris's way of teaching us and bumping up our low grades at the same time. Looking down at my sheet of paper and flipping through my science book like it was a race to see who can finish first, I saw a couple drops of water fall onto my quiz, then another, then another. As I looked up and wiped my forehead; the terrifying moment wasn't seeing a tremendous amount of sweat dripping off my fingertips, it was not being able to feel me wipe my hand on my forehead. I couldn't feel a thing, and at that moment my body was completely numb. April Stanton was a cheerleader who sat in front of me in fifth period, always looking in the mirror and doing her make-up. She slightly turned the mirror in my direction reaching for her make-up bag and I saw a complete ghost. My face was dripping with sweat and I wasn't even hot (or couldn't feel that I was hot anyway), my face was pale, and my cheeks were light purple. I looked around the room and nobody even noticed what was going on. Mrs. Harris always read her Nicholas Sparks books while we took a test or quiz, so I knew she wasn't paying any attention. Time was wasting, and I needed to finish my quiz but I couldn't function. The paper was soaked with sweat at this point and I tried picking it up and waving it around to dry the wet spots, but it was getting difficult to grip it by the second. It dropped immediately on the floor next to me and when I made an attempt to reach down and pick it up, my body shut down and I collapsed onto the floor, again making a connection with the side of a desk like a flashback of my incident with Billy Clayton as a kid... only I couldn't feel this one. Lying flat on my back, all I saw was a blurred vision of Todd and Mrs. Harris looking down at me. They were speaking but I couldn't hear anything coming out of their mouths.

Apparently I passed out because the next thing I knew, I woke up in a bright yellow room and Dr. Browden standing over me with his long white robe on and his thick pair of glasses he only wears when his contacts irritates him. "So glad you can join us

Mr. Treyton. No don't move you'll yank the cords out!" I felt like I was strapped to the bed seeing all these tubes and cords attached to my body, but the good thing is at least I was feeling something. The fingers in my hands came back and I was thinking about checking my forehead until Dr. Browden snapped at me.

"Where are Mom and Dad?" I asked, and he told me they were getting drinks from the cafeteria and they would be right back. I don't know if it was just in my head but my fingers felt better than they have before. I couldn't explain it in words really, but Dr. Browden was talking away about why it happened. Something about blood flow, but I wasn't really paying any attention. You would think I would want to listen since my life was almost at risk, but for some odd reason I kept moving my fingers around strangely like I was doing sign language. My parents were approaching the door and Dr. Browden took them out in the hall to talk to them. My Mom was peeking through the Plexiglas at the door and I gave her my, "I want to hear" face. What were they talking about?

There was something they weren't telling me, and I was going to find out what it was sooner or later.

The ride home was very quiet. I didn't really notice for the first ten minutes because I was still wiggling my fingers around, and Dad kept looking at me through the rearview mirror. So I decided to break the ice.

"So what's for dinner?" I asked.

"Your mom's not cooking tonight, so we'll run by subway and grab us something." Dad said. It felt extremely awkward in the car, and it made me think it was something Dr. Browden said to shake them up. I wasn't nervous at all. My body felt amazing, and if I had feeling in my legs, I felt like I could run for miles! Todd called when I got home to check on me and see how I was doing. He wanted details about what the doctor said, but all I could tell him was how amazing and free I felt. My brothers came into my room and checked on me as well. "Aye cuz, you ai'ight?" Mason swore he was from the hood and I had to remind him every day that we went to a private school. "Yeah Bro, I'm doing well now." I said.

CHAPTER EIGHT

I would usually take a small nap after school but, I was passed wide awake. I knew I was a bit hyper when I caught myself cleaning my room. As I was wiping down my windows I saw the neighbors next door bringing their last few boxes into their home, and then noticed a familiar face. Dark hair, green eyes, and a smile that could light up a city at night. The new girl that took my seat. Last time she saw me I was laying on my back unconscious. If I didn't make a good impression on her when she last saw me I know she had dismissed my existence by this time, but what did I have to lose? I strolled through the hallway, into the kitchen and my mom was making brownies. My mom was a health nut (as people like to call her) so if we ever saw her baking anything that had sugar in it, we knew it wasn't for us. Unless it was Christmas or Thanksgiving, then she would make me my own pumpkin pie, but that's another story.

"So who are the brownies for?" I asked. No matter how old you get there's just something about licking the bowl that everyone likes. So I waited right there next to her until she scraped all the chocolate into the pan. "They're for your neighbors next door, so when these brownies are done tell one of your brothers to take them over there and welcome them to the neighborhood."

"Okay I will." More like I won't, tell my brothers that is. That was kind of a perfect opportunity. One of those moments you don't get a lot and one I couldn't afford to miss or mess up. So naturally I decided to take them over myself, but before I went, I needed to practice. I needed to go over my lines as to what I'm going to say when I get over there. "HEY!" No that's too loud; she might think I'm coming on too strong. *"Um hi, how are you?"* hmm, no that's too proper, I need to be a little bit smoother and cool. So I kept practicing in the mirror trying to get my facial expressions, tone, and what to say down before I went over. I smelled the brownies in the oven already and knew it was getting closer to game time.

After the brownies were baked and cooled off, I went over there and rang the doorbell. Her mom answered the door and I couldn't have been more disappointed, but I had to fake it. I tried to peak through the door to see if she was anywhere in sight, but I saw nothing but a little toy poodle in a miniature Alabama football Jersey. Just ridiculous.

"Hi I'm Alex; these are from the Treyton family here next door. Just wanted to welcome you and your family to the neighborhood." Nailed it. I hope this helps me in some way.

"Well hi there, I'm Kathy and they smell wonderful, thank you."

"You're welcome, nice to meet you Mrs. Kathy." Trying to be inconspicuous, I peeked through the door again to see if she was anywhere in sight. No sign of her. Oh well, at least I planted a seed with Mrs. Kathy. Hopefully my name will pop up in conversation in their house, and she'll soon notice me. As I left their house I heard the door open back up. "Hey" I turned around and there she was. Even beautiful without make-up on.

"Hey" I said, keeping it simple because my practice in the mirror was not a success and was cut short due to the challenge of finding a different outfit to wear that might impress her. She came outside in shorts, a tank-top, and her hair pulled back and I was still amazed by her natural beauty. Noticeably staring, she distinctively picked up on me looking her up and down and quickly showed signs of insecurity.

"I usually dress nicer, but I didn't know anyone was stopping by, so I just came out to..." cutting her off smoothly "Are you kidding me, you look great, I was just stopping by to give you and your family brownies. Just a, you know, a welcome to the neighborhood sorta thing."

She looked at me with a slight grin, "Oh, well that's sweet of you. By the way about earlier today...what was that about?" Immediately I felt embarrassed. I wanted to change the subject quick, but I had to give her something. I told her I was fine and pretty much had the same conversation with her that I did with Todd. She felt concerned and wanted to know what caused it and wanted to know if there was anything she could do. I could tell she was a little confounded that I didn't really take it serious and kept going on about how awesome my hands felt. I told her not to worry, and that I feel even better than before.

Then she tells me that "people like me" are usually in the loop on what's going on with their bodies, and that, "in my condition" I should listen to the doctor more. Normal me would have been excited that she even talked to me; let alone be concerned about me but in this case I felt attacked. Like 'I'm the poor crippled boy who can't function and needs medical attention immediately before I die in two weeks' kind of attacked.   I'm no charity case you know. And for some reason those exact same words just dribbled out of mouth before I could catch them.

"I'm not a charity case you know."

"I know you're not I didn't mean it like that."

"Well that's how it sounded." I said.

"Well I'm sorry, okay?" she says.

"What do you know about me anyway? You know nothing! So don't worry about my "disability" as you like to call it, because I'm going to be fine." I caught myself breathing heavy and started to settle down. Maybe she was right. Maybe I do need to take it seriously and listen to my doctor. My parents usually handled the bad news. They really didn't want me knowing a lot of details so I wouldn't be stressed at a young age, and I understood that fully. Then again, it is my body so I should want to know why things are happening. But it seemed like my doctor and my parents had some type of agreement. I took a deep breath and we both just stood there in the awkward silence. She kept running her fingers through her bangs while I rolled my wheel chair back and forth a little. She found out my nervous habit and I found hers, and everything became calm after we took a moment.

"I'm sorry" I said.

Then she looked up at me with those green eyes, and puzzled face, "Well, I'm sorry I cared." Then she walked back in her house and slammed the door. Well that went well. I just pissed off the beautiful new girl in my 1st period class that is also my neighbor.

The next day wasn't so great either. We were partnered together for a science project and I ended up catching her hair on fire by accident. Just the tip got burned but, she freaked out like any normal girl would do. A week had past and we hadn't said two words to each other or even looked in each other's direction while passing in the halls. I thought we'd never talk again even though it was just a silly little argument. I got over it, but her not so much it seemed, and I'm sure part of it was the whole science class thing. I apologized heavily for that and you couldn't even tell anything was damaged. She even had a little smirk on her face as if she wanted to laugh about it, but wanted to keep a straight face to prove a point. I thought we'd never talk again after I screwed that up, but Mrs. Harris assigned us another project together and immediately Venessa tried to switch partners.

"I'm not working with him Mrs. Harris, he set my hair on fire!!" Mrs. Harris totally had my back on this one, but also pointed out the fact that I needed to be more careful.

"I told you to put your hair up before we did the procedure, did I not? And Alex just please be more careful next time." She did have long hair, and with the length it was, it was bound to get caught into something sooner or later. Venessa looked at her with her mouth wide open, "Whatever, let's just get this over with." I had no clue how this was going to pan out but I just had in my mind to go with the flow and get it over with. Our assignment was to find out if smoke in the air affects plant transpiration, and show it, so we knew if we wanted a good grade we had to put our differences aside for the time being. We decided to meet at my place at 5:30pm and start on the research part of it when we got out of school.

My parents normally go for their two mile run three nights a week so they leave the dinner in the oven for me to attack, and they leave when the weather gets cool around 5:00 pm. As they walk out the door my mom yells, "Aleeexxx, compannny!" Company?! I looked out one of bedroom windows on the second level which is right above the front door and see my parents letting Venessa in the door while they're on their way out. She was thirty minutes early and I still haven't taken a shower yet because I was too busy playing NCAA on my Xbox. I smelled my armpit. It wasn't bad but it could have been fresher. I took off my shirt and grabbed another t-shirt quickly from my drawer and put it on.

"Alex, You up There?" Venessa called from below.

"Yeah, come on up!" I crawled from my wheelchair onto my bed and just sat there with the laptop in my lap as she walked in, and I was just sitting there with a blank stare on my face trying to hide the heavy breathing from trying to get myself together. "You okay?" she asked.

"Yeah I'm fine." I said.

"Alright well let's do this then." She seemed cooled down from what I can tell but a sudden spark could definitely start the fire again, so I was trying to play it safe. She took her laptop out and we started the research part of our project. My laptop was being extremely slow so I just set it to the side. It seemed pretty awkward at first because we both felt the tension in the room, and I felt like I was breathing down her neck, peaking over her shoulder trying to look at her screen. It went better than I thought it was going to go and we ended up actually getting some work done without killing each other, or her just killing me.

We decided to meet again the following night at the same time, and after that night we just made it a routine until the project was complete. The more time we spent together, the more I actually started to appreciate her personality. It was like I finally understood her. After the art project and the time spent together, Venessa and I still spoke and strangely became closer whether we wanted to realize it or not. We would laugh and carry on a conversation for a good thirty minutes before we realized we were bonding too much, then she would look down at her watch then say goodbye.

I went for my weekly check-up a few days later and finally decided to take Venessa's advice and ask Dr. Browden more questions about my body. "So how are ya feeling Alex?"

"Well, a lot better since the incident."

"Good, good, I'm glad to hear that." he says.

"I'm a little nervous to ask, but I just want to know a little more about what these check-ups are for, ya know? Like, why my body reacted the way it did that day, and I know I barely pay attention to what you say, but I would like to know now." I say. He sits down to think about it. "Alex." he says, rubbing his head. "The things I leave out are for your protection, trust me. Your parents and I care about you a lot and we just want you to know that we are trying in every way to keep you healthy and happy." he says. He gets up and leans down to give me a hug. "Can you accept that buddy?"

"I can." I wasn't too worried only because my parents trusted him like he was their father, so naturally I just fell into place. I always had a lot on my mind at that time, thinking about the future, what I was going to do with my life, and will I ever find that love of my life. Also having a few new feelings, feelings I never really thought about until I became older. Lately wondering why I'm so different from the rest of my family. Not just because of my disability, but a certain disconnect I couldn't put my finger on. It haunted me, and I knew my parents would be saddened to know I felt that way. I went to a specific place to clear my head and just be alone for a few hours. It's good to get away from the madness of the world every once in a while.

On the beautiful days when the sun was shining, the wind was blowing just right and the temperature was perfect I would go to this place. This place was surrounded in trees, enormous flat rocks you can just sprawl out on. It got me through a lot and through the years of living in Alabama, just being in that place made things more clear, or so I thought. I always told my parents I wanted to travel, and go someplace that I've never been before. They loved the fact that I was open to different things and not so closed minded. They were all about supporting my dreams and ambitions anyway they could and whether they knew or not, I saw it and appreciated it greatly.

I moved through time with a growing circle of people I could trust and love and I survived the new move, the new school and all the ups and downs with my body in between. When my eighteenth birthday came around I woke up feeling all grown up. I even went and checked my face in the mirror to see if my sideburns were coming in thicker. They weren't. I rolled into the bathroom and lying right next to my toothbrush were two tickets. Two plane tickets to Europe. I couldn't believe it! I went to my parent's bedroom right away and hugged their necks and thanked them. I asked how they got the tickets at a good price, and who the other ticket was for. Dad said a gentleman at his work just gave them to him, and thought it would be perfect for me to experience at my age. What a clever man, whoever he was. Plus, I could take anyone I'd like on the trip with me. I called Venessa and asked if she would go and she ran right over just to hug me tight. She seemed more excited than I was about it all. We grew real close over the years. That crush was definitely still there, but since I knew she didn't feel the same I never brought it up.

CHAPTER NINE

We packed immediately and headed for the airport the following week. Our parents were there to see us off, and making sure we made it on our flight okay. I was ready for Europe. I love their style, their food, and the accents. My style of dress would blend in pretty well. V-neck, fitted jeans, long beanie, and Chuck Taylors, and that's on a chill day. Venessa and I both slept through most of the flight and when I woke up about an hour before landing and I was feeling a little sick from eating all the snacks earlier.

Venessa was still knocked out and snoring just loud enough to rule out it being heavy breathing. This Asian guy sitting behind us to the right, with a tattoo of a Chinese symbol on his face, kept on glancing our way. I'm not sure if that was his way of saying, "please shut her up" or what, but it was a little creepy to say the least. The plane was about to land and Venessa was coming out of her coma.

"Sleep well?" I asked.

She gave me that look people give when they haven't

totally waken up yet. "Yeah, I was so tired. Are we there yet?" she asked as she yawned real big.

"Yeah we're about to land." We started to gather our things and waited for the plane to stop. Looking outside at the beautiful architecture, the anticipation of exploring the different cities was strong and the look on Venessa's face was probably the same look I had on mine. We looked at each other and just laughed with excitement. When we got inside the airport to get our luggage, Venessa couldn't seem to wait patiently because she was full of anticipation and energy. She started pushing me around in my wheelchair, and twirling me around all over the place. I was sitting there laughing hysterically while everyone just stared awkwardly.

We finally grabbed our bags and headed outside to grab a taxi. Such beautiful weather and we were in a hurry to tour the city. Venessa brought flash cards with her to help her pick up on certain words and phrases people would say. When we got in the taxi it smelled like someone poured a jar of pickles on the floor, and the taxi driver was talking so fast and we didn't even understand what he was saying. Thanks to Venessa's flash cards she interpreted some of the words to me so I understood the gist of what he was saying. Otherwise I would have just been nodding my head and smiling like I always do when I didn't hear someone the first time.

We drove into the city of Belgium and it was amazing. There was so much diversity and culture-- very different from Alabama that's for sure. Venessa wanted to get out and take pictures with the statues every time we passed by one. Then she would yell out the window, "I love Europe!" I would just laugh and I'm sure the taxi driver comes across tourist like us all the time which is probably the reason he was so calm. We pulled up to our hotel and it was gorgeous. My parents went all out and put us in the Marriot, and it was really close to the water. I was so excited I was trying to get out of the car before grabbing my wheelchair. Venessa started to laugh after I almost fell out of the car. The doorman came out with a big grin on his face.

"Hi, I'm Cole. Here let me help you guys. That's why

I'm here ya know. Oh, and to make your stay here at the beautiful Marriot hotel pleasant." He says. He was a skinny middle aged man who was extremely perky. His hair covered up his forehead almost reaching his eyes. He brushed it to the side every other minute. He grabbed all three bags which were pretty heavy, and even though he struggled a bit that was impressive for a guy his size.

Before we get very far he is stopped by the recognition of someone and he yells out in surprise. "Derek! What are you doing here?" Cole asks happily as he sets the bags down.

"I thought I told you I'd be back in town this week. I'm helping open up that new café over there on Court Street remember?" Derek says.

"Oh yea that's right I forgot! Congratulations," Cole says hugging him.

"So who do we have here? Derek asks staring at Venessa. I'm not even sure he knew I was in the room by the way he glared at her.

"Hi, I'm Venessa and this is my friend Alex. We're visiting from Alabama." She says.

"Wow, a long way from home aren't we"? Cole says.

"I knew you weren't from around here. I know everyone in this town or at least have seen them before. I would have remembered those beautiful eyes. Those are a pair of eyes you don't forget." Derek says smiling while Venessa blushes.

"Well I'm going to help take their bags to their room, I'll call you later." Cole says.

"Sounds good man, take care of these two…especially Ms. Venessa. Hope you guys have a good stay here, and make sure you check out my restaurant Café Louista on Court Street!" Derek says as he winks at Venessa.

We walked in the door to our roommate style apartment and it was incredible! The two words to describe it would have to be classy and elegant, just my style. I didn't want to unpack yet, I was too eager to get out and see the city but Venessa's a neat freak and insisted that we unpack first so we don't have to do it when we get back. This might sound like me being a girl, but the closet space was just what I needed. My shoe bag that I brought was bigger than my suitcase with my clothes in it, and all my shoes stayed clean for the simple fact that I don't walk around, but I would take care of them either way. If I don't do anything else I just want to look good, all the time.

We finally unpacked and were ready to hit the city. My mother kept calling every hour making sure I was okay, and making it very clear that I needed to be back by Friday. Thoughts were going through my mind like, 'what if I wanted to stay longer? What if I fell in love with the place and decided I want to live in Europe?' I sure didn't want to stay in Alabama all my life. Venessa was getting the same phone calls from her dad telling her make sure she puts on sun block so she doesn't burn, and hinting that she better not have TOO much fun with any boys. I whispered in his ear before we left that I would make sure she didn't. He winked and said, "Adda boy."

Venessa and I went to this pizza place across the street from our hotel first before we went on this grand tour of the city that we scheduled earlier. We ordered a large sausage pizza and I must say, the taxis may have been small but their pizzas were not. I looked at Venessa and she was sitting across from me in the booth working on her second slice.

"Alex I'll be right back, I have to go to the bathroom" she said as she slid out of the booth sucking her fingers from pizza sauce. Todd and I had been emailing back and forth randomly throughout the day. We had this game we played where we would quote lines from movies and whoever runs out first loses. We were both movie buffs so neither of us ever ran out really, things just came up or one of us had to go to work so we had to put the game on hold for the time being. Still best friends since my first year at Brentwood, and nothing's changed with us except for facial hair and a few near death experiences of his eating the wrong foods causing his allergies to act up in the worse way possible. If there was one thing he hated in his life it was peanuts. It almost took him out on his 16th birthday when his girlfriend's mother brought peanut butter cupcakes to the party. Enough said. He had to be monitored closely ever since then and his parents would not let him go on this trip with me in fear that something might happen without them being present. They trusted me in many ways, but I understand them not taking a chance with his life.

He was emailing me how much he wanted to go and telling me what Venessa and I should do while we were there. We lost track of time and had to get the rest of our pizza to-go. "Should we leave a tip?" She asks.

"Well we paid before we sat down so I don't know." I said. "I'll leave a few dollars just in case," she says and tosses a few dollars on the table and I noticed they were doodled upon.

"Smiley faces? Really?" I said.

"What?" she says giggling, "I put them on all my dollars. I always do it just in case I purchase something and one winds up back in my hands, it's the coolest thing!" she says. The little things tickled her.

"Has it ever happened before?" I asked.

"Not yet, but if I do it long enough it's bound to happen one of these days. You should try it! Just don't put a smiley face because that's my thing."

"Haha very funny. I'll put a frowny face, how's that?"
I said jokingly.

CHAPTER TEN

Excited about the day we rushed outside squinting while being greeted by the bright sun. It was time for our grand tour of the city and Venessa still had it in her mind to take pictures by the statues. While waiting for the rest of the group to show up that was obviously late, in fact that we showed up late ourselves, our tour guide asked us where we were from and what made us want to come. Then after we answered there was that awkward silence as if he didn't know what else to ask, and when that happens it's just best to act like you're texting. The rest of the tourists finally showed up and we started to walk around the city. It was a two hour tour and everyone were taking turns pushing me in my wheelchair; having much more fun than expected. Big buildings, and statues with a lot of history behind them intrigued us and it made me like the place even more.

As the tour guide was talking about a particular statue, across the street was a little souvenir shop and in the window was a shirt that said, "I left my heart in the Swiss Alps." Venessa was determined to get it and despite the fact that we were gonna be in the area an entire week, she ran over swiftly while dodging a taxi on the way. Not even a minute later she comes back out of the store with a confused look on her face, shifting her eyes in every direction. I came over to see what the problem was while the guide and the others kept on walking.

"What's wrong?" I asked, as her eyes still shifted everywhere and her body language screaming 'nervous wreck'.

She sputtered out: "I... I don't have my purse! Have you seen my purse, I just had my purse!"

Seeing as though we walked everywhere we went and had not stopped in any stores during the tour before this point, my only logical explanation was it had to be where we were last. She must have left it at the pizza place. We did rush out of there pretty fast and I didn't remember her having it on her during the tour. We didn't even tell the tour guide we were leaving; we just took off full speed down the street. Venessa grabbed the handles on my wheelchair firmly and pushed off starting with a medium jog. She started to speed up at one point and my left wheel hit a rock almost catapulting me onto the pavement. I couldn't blame her though, I'm sure I'd be the same way. We finally get to Pizzaros and we surged in straight to the booth where we were sitting. Nothing was there.

"Did you find a purse in this booth at all ma'am!?" Venessa asked the cashier and looking around aimlessly she told us she hadn't seen it. She runs into the bathroom, then comes storming out looking under chairs and booths in the restaurant once again.

"I don't think it's here...anymore that is" I tell her. Still searching high and low, eyes watering, and mood shifted she gets up off the floor and walks out of the restaurant. I pushed open the door and put my hand on her back.

"Alex, what are we going to do?"

"I don't know. I'm pretty sure it's been stolen so we should probably go to the police and see what they can do." As we headed down the street we tried to figure out what the emergency contact number for Europe was, or if it was even different from 911.

It was nothing but a night of constant disappointment. No help from police and everyone we came in contact with didn't care to help. Not only did Venessa lose her purse but we lost our tickets back to Alabama, all of our money, hotel key, and her cell phone. Luckily we had mine to keep in touch with our family, without it I couldn't because I haven't memorized any of their numbers. We searched everywhere, using the last of the money we had in our pockets for a cab to drive us around. Still nothing. Dark clouds filled the sky. It was sticky and muggy out, and as the sun disappeared into the clouds we still felt the harsh humidity. The weather was affecting both of our moods. Venessa was getting irritable and tired, nodding off in the cab. We hadn't eaten in hours since Pizzaros. I can go a while without eating. Liquids can hold me for a while, and the large cup of lemonade lasted pretty long. Venessa on the other hand was struggling. The cab dropped us back off at the hotel and we just sat on the front steps for a minute.

"What are we going to do?" She asked.

"I don't know. We'll think of something. It could be

worse I suppose." I said. I spoke too soon. As we sat there I felt a few drops of cold rain hit my neck sending chills down my back. Then it started to pour. Venessa was struggling with my chair, trying to pull it up the steps. Her little muscles must have been exhausted, and I know the sun had beat both of us down from hours of searching. We were getting soaked. I felt her give up, and as I started to drift downward a guy ran up and grabbed the handlebars. "I got it!" He said. He dropped his bag on the steps, leaving it to get soaked as he pulled me into the doorway. "You guys okay?" Venessa stood there in silence staring at the floor.

"Yes, we're fine bro, thanks a lot for the help." I said. I could tell she was not in the mood for conversation even though he was nice enough to do what he did. "Any time man. By the way I'm Tyler. I stay in those apartments right across the bridge." He said.

"Oh, okay cool bro. I'm Alex and this is Venessa." She was still looking down. "Sorry, she's a bit tired right now; we're about to head up the elevator to go crash if you don't mind." I added. No not at all man, you guys do your thing." He said.

We let the front desk know that we lost our keycard and he gave us a new one after making sure we were in the data base. "Wait!" Tyler says. He takes a hotel business card off the front desk and writes on the back of it. "Here is my number, you know...if you guys need anything. Don't hesitate to call." He said walking towards the door.

"Thanks will do. Take care man and thanks again!" I said. We finally got upstairs to our room and just looking at our beds made us both smile. We immediately put on clean, dry clothes and lay down in our beds cooling off by the air conditioning vent blowing full blast.

After years of catering to Venessa, and being at her beck and call, I realized it became simply second nature at this point. Falling in love with a girl was one of my strong points; that was always easy to do for me, but a girl falling in love with me seemed like an unending journey of disappointment. Not being the jock in school would have made me invisible if not for my witty comments I would randomly spurt out in the middle of class just for a chuckle. Venessa always laughed at my jokes the loudest. Coming into class and seeing her for the first time, my heart dropped, and I never pursued anyone else for fear that deep down she might actually have feelings for me. The way she looked at me, and the way she treated me was some type of feeling and care for me that I couldn't describe by telling anyone. I can never tell her. Our first encounter didn't start off great, but after spending a certain amount of time with someone, it's hard to deny a distinctive connection. We both fell sound asleep almost as soon as we hit our pillows.

The weather was shifty the next morning, raining off and on. Venessa even woke up a little sore. I suppose from all the walking and pushing me around all day. We decided to order some wings, and stay in for a bit to watch TV. Wings for breakfast weren't exactly our first choice but a coupon for eighteen free wings was as good as it was going to get at the moment. We didn't plan on being inside the hotel the entire day because we were still on the hunt to find her purse. If we didn't end up finding it by tomorrow we were going to have to come clean to the parents, and maybe never be trusted to go anywhere alone again. So that was our last resort. Hearing the rain outside made both of us drowsy, and I wasn't about to have a rerun of yesterday happen again. I know Venessa wasn't.

"We should probably look for my purse shouldn't we?" she said tiredly. I rolled over on my side so I was facing her. "Yeah...we should." Neither one of us moved a muscle. Instead we sat there in silence for about fifteen minutes. Then we heard a knock at the door that startled us both. "Wings!" Venessa yells. She hops out of bed and runs to the door. Where did she get all of this energy out of nowhere from? I still didn't move a muscle. Of course she would have beaten me to the door regardless. She opens the door and it's not the wing guy with our food, it's Tyler. He's breathing heavily leaning against the door holding a bag. It was her purse. "Oh my goodness!" Venessa's yells as her face lights up. "Where did you find it?!" she asked. She hugged him tight before he could even get a word out. A little jealousy stirred up in me. I wanted to be the one to find it. I wanted her to hug me tight and appreciate me. Then she might actually have a reason to like me. That sounded weird even saying it in my mind. What was I so jealous about anyway, I should be happy he found the purse. He came inside. Venessa was still jumping up and down, clapping her hands together like a hyper seal. I still didn't know where she found this energy from, and I don't know how Tyler got the purse back either.

He sat down on the bed to catch his breath. He started to tell us the entire story, but I can't get into a story unless you're acting it out and Venessa was busy looking through her purse making sure everything was there. "The money! All the money is gone!" she yells.

"You really didn't expect it to still be there did you? I mean, I'd just be glad the tickets, cell phone, and everything else is still in there," Tyler said.

We shouldn't have been carrying all that cash around the city anyway. Reminds me of the first week my brothers and I got allowance and mom told me to only bring twenty dollars out of the one hundred dollars they had given me. Of course I didn't listen and stuffed all the bills in my pocket before we left for the mall. It was extra windy that day and being paranoid, I kept sticking my hands in my pockets to make sure the money was still in place. All it took was one time for me to take my hands out of my tight pockets pulling the bills out, as I did so I watched a few twenties fly in the air. Surprisingly enough, they didn't give me a whooping that day. A worse punishment was watching the rest of the family shop and I didn't have much left to spend on anything remotely worthwhile.

We were definitely grateful for Tyler finding Venessa's purse and what was even better was his insistence on showing us the rest of the city on his dime. It was more than a generous offer and Venessa and I just quickly glanced at each other and smiled. "So I take that as a yes then." Tyler says. "I'll come by and get you guys before noon and I will show you all the beautiful sites!" he adds.

This was exciting. We felt like our vacation was finally starting. "Well I guess we can stay in the rest of the day!" Venessa says. As if we were going to find the motivation to get out of our beds to go in to town and search for her purse anyway. I can tell you now it wasn't going to happen. There was a knock at the door again and this time it was the wings. I honestly felt bad that we didn't have any money to tip the guy, but we were so hungry we started to feel sorrier for ourselves. There's something about a cloudy, rainy day that makes you lazy and tired. The feeling that makes you not want to do anything but stay inside surrounded by junk food and curled up under your blanket watching movies all day. Then there's the days when you wake up and the sun streams through the blinds and gives you that boost of energy to get up and save the world. Or just leave the house. Venessa came over to my bedside and sat next to me.

"What's the matter?" She asked. My mind was racing, as I sat there in deep thought. "Nothing I'm fine. It's just, he reminds me of someone." I say.

"Who Tyler?"

"Yes." I say.

"Well everyone has a familiar face of someone we know. Let's get some sleep so we can be ready for an awesome day tomorrow, okay." She says.

"Alright." I felt a bit weird as I got ready for bed. I didn't know why. I had to get some sleep so I blocked it out. I turned off the lamp next to me, and pulled the covers over me.

CHAPTER ELEVEN

Tyler picked us up at exactly eleven thirty. He had a long list with him of all the places we were going, and Venessa and I were stoked. I spend some of the driving time on the phone with my parents just checking in and seeing how everything was going. Apparently Dr. Browden's test had come back. It turned out he was poisoned. The Chemical still couldn't be identified, but I was just glad he was okay. Venessa was on the phone also, but her conversations were a bit different. Her parents were just looking out for her, making sure she was safe and she knew how to look out for herself. She took offense to it, thinking they had the idea that she wasn't smart enough to know better. Communication issues of the family always got carried over into the hotel room and I received an ear full every night about how they don't trust her and she's old enough to make her own decisions without being checked on every second of the day.

She started again in the car and I had to change the

subject before she got on her soap box. "Nice car bro. I wonder how many duckets it took to get this baby!" I say. Tyler drove a brand new Porsche. Leather interior, black on the inside and silver on the outside, my mouth dropped when I walked out the door but I tried to keep my composure. His family is obviously loaded so it made me feel better about his splurging on us the entire day. "Thanks man, yeah I just got it. I sold my old one not too long ago, but I'm definitely keeping this one." he says. I wanted to ask him what his parents do for a living. Or what he does for a living, but I didn't want to pry. Venessa seemed quite fond of the car herself, playing with the radio and touching and turning every knob that she didn't know what it did. I could tell Tyler didn't like it, but he didn't say anything.

There were too many beautiful sites to count, and so much time to kill. We went everywhere, ate everything, and Tyler went all out on buying us souvenirs and t-shirts for when we went back home - even shirts for our family, as if finding the purse and taking us around the city wasn't enough. Too many cabs there too, while Alabama had none - none that I ever saw. People crossing the road without looking or caring if a car is coming. Total chaos. Outside the city we visited a place called the meadows where Tyler went as a little boy with his parents. Nothing to do on the ride but think, passing mountains and terrain, blooming flowers everywhere and an old abandoned church surrounded by weeds. It was quiet. As peaceful as the place I always went to back home to get away.

"I use to lay right here and my parents use to read books to me all the time...they seem too busy to come these days now that I'm older. Tyler says.

"Well at least all their hard work landed you a Porsche. What teenager can say that?" I say. Venessa nods her head in agreement.

"Having money doesn't compare to having a family. It feels like all I have is memories now, and I'm sure the two of you never knew what that felt like." he says. The mood shifted quickly. It was obvious I hit a nerve. "No man, you're right...I don't. I apologize." I say. I don't like confrontation, so any chance I get to shift the mood back to a positive vibe was my mission in these situations. He said nothing. It was too awkward to change the subject right off the back so we waited in silence. He parked and went to sit down on the steps of the old church and Venessa followed. "You can always get those moments back you know. You just have to tell them how you feel, that's all." she says.

"I don't think so." he states. The two gazed off into the beautiful scenery looking out at the mountains, and watching the wind softly move the flowers. She slowly reached over and grabbed his hand. He was looking the other way, but a peaceful smile came over his face. Again a little jealousy came over me as I tried to think maybe she was just comforting him. Maybe it meant nothing. Surely she can't be developing feelings for him. We'll be leaving in three days so it wouldn't do any good anyhow. He turns to her, and puts his arm around her, "If only I could get those days back. Times are different now. Everyone is different now." he says.

It started to thunder and what once was a beautiful

blue sky started to turn grey. "We better go before it rains." I said, mostly trying to stop the moment going on between the two, but a good enough reason to not make me appear jealous. "Yeah we'd better go." she says. Right before reaching the car Tyler runs back over by the church and grabs a few wild flowers out of the ground and hands them to her. The smile on her face was so wide, and she gave him a big hug that lasted long enough for rain drops to start falling on our heads. I was just waiting for him to unlock the door, but their little romance seemed more important to them. She sat in the front seat on the way back home. I felt like the third wheel which wasn't remotely new to me. It felt like someone just interrupted my date and took my girl home, with me left sitting in the back seat while they held hands the whole way back. We took a different way back to the hotel which seemed longer. Or maybe it was just me. So many thoughts going through my head it was hard to process it all. It started to pour down rain and the road we were on was gravely and bumpy. I shifted in my seat a few times sliding into the window.

"You okay back there Alex?" Tyler asks. I got myself together to answer him as if nothing bothered me. "Yeah, I'm fine bro, thanks." I say. He walked her into the lobby and they both stood there not saying a word, just kind of stared into each other's eyes. I assumed they were waiting on me to be out of site so they could kiss, so I just made up an excuse to go ahead and head up to the room without her. Even though the thought of them kissing made me dry heave.

"I'm a little tired so I'm going to go ahead and head to the room. I'll see you up there in a bit Venessa." I say. "Okay, I'll be right behind you." she says. "It was fun man, thanks for hanging out." Tyler says. I tried to crack a smile but it was a struggle, but the muscles in my face finally allowed it. "Thanks for everything man, I had fun too." I headed up the elevator and tears fell down my face. This always happens to me. Why did I think I had a shot anyway? I planned on ignoring her when she came back to the room, but at the same time acting like everything was ok. I was good at that. Practice makes perfect, and I've had a lot of it. I lay in bed waiting for the door knob to move, but it never did.

Lying there under the sheets made me tired and I struggled to stay awake, and ended up falling asleep before she came up. My dream was normal. It was just like any other dream I suppose, but not like the few I've had before. I woke up in the middle of it to a bang on the door. I figured Venessa had lost her key, and hopped in my chair to get the door. When I opened it there was no one there. I looked both ways down the hall and still no sight of anyone. As I turned around to go back inside, I haphazardly looked down and found a note lying right outside the door. I picked it up and it read, *"Remember. Remember or it's too late."* My heart leaped. I peaked around the corner again to make sure no one was watching me. I felt someone there but still saw no one. Unsettled, I went back inside and got in bed. Turned on my side staring at the note on the night stand, I couldn't help but to be a little disturbed. Who would write such a thing and leave it on my doorstep? Was it even left for me? What would it mean if it was? These are the questions that were going through my head. It was getting late and my mind was still racing, but after while I found myself dreaming again.

CHAPTER TWELVE

The next morning I woke up and Venessa wasn't in her bed. The sick thought of her sleeping over at Tyler's place made me nauseous. Then I found a note lying beside me saying, "Sorry I didn't get to see you this morning. I went to the museum with Tyler, I'll be back soon." Who knew I'd end up losing my best friend on my birthday trip. I would sulk all day like I normally would do, and feel sorry for myself. After a while that just seemed to add to the embarrassment and make things worse. She wasn't going to find me in the hotel watching MTV when she came back that's for sure. Instead I was going on my own journey through the city, and maybe meet someone myself. I got dressed immediately. Heading down the elevator I was pondering where I was going to go. Who knew? I was just going to go. The money that Tyler gave us each was more than what we had before, and with tomorrow being our last day, I decided to go all out. I finally got a cab after the last three rudely drove past me with no passengers inside.

"Can you just drive for now? I'll tell you when to stop please." The cab driver just shrugged his shoulders. "Whatever you say friend." he says. I can admit I wasn't too confident about going out on my own. I was a little scared actually, but once I got out and about I was fine. I just felt like taking a drive I guess, get out of the hotel. My mind was clouded with so many things; I needed this to somehow feel like an actual vacation. Like yesterday. Thinking too much had me not paying attention, and unaware of where I was. When I started to see fewer buildings around me I noticed I wasn't in the city anymore. Little houses and more land with donkeys and goats.

"Sir, sir can we turn around please, I'm sorry." I said.

"Where do you want to go?" The driver asked, staring me down in the rear view mirror. "There are other people that actually have somewhere to be I can be assisting right now, but it's your money so do what you like." he says. I felt a little hostility in his voice. He turns around and drives for a few miles, still in unfamiliar territory. I was in the need of some adventure but just didn't know what. "You know what. Just drop me off right here." I said sternly. He didn't expect that. "Where will you go? Not too many cabs around here my friend, I'll drive you back." He says. "Just let me out!" I may have startled him when I hit the back of the passenger seat with my fist as I yelled at him causing him to slam on the breaks. "Get out then, just get out!" he yells. I threw some money in the back seat without counting it or looking at the meter for how much I owed him, grabbed my chair and managed my way out as he spun away.

I probably gave him more than I owed, but oh well. Probably not the best move since looking around I didn't see too much transportation around. He was right. No cabs around here at all. My phone was at thirty five percent, and I left my charger with Venessa. A goat walked across the road and I knew I was in no man's land. As always I can mind the sun but humidity I can't take. Not with the long sleeve shirt I had on, but at the time it seemed like a good idea, mainly because my cold nature couldn't take the temperature in the hotel. I sat there for a second and text Venessa to see how her adventure with wonder boy was going. No response. I didn't expect to see a cab drive by anytime soon, and hitching a ride from a total stranger was out of the question.

So there I was, stranded. Adventure was always an item on my bucket list, but I wasn't sure I wanted it like this. If I don't come back Venessa will be worried and call me. I kept glancing at my phone battery percentage. What if I'm out here long enough for it to die? How will she contact me then? I thought long and hard what my next step was. If I wasn't so stubborn and just let the cab driver take me back, I wouldn't be in this predicament. Of course leaving in the first place was pointless in itself, but something in me always thinks I need to prove a point. What point? I haven't figured that out yet, but the main thing I needed to figure out was how am I going to get back to the hotel. There was a small cottage in the distance with an old car parked out front, maybe someone is home that can help. Someone that won't kidnap me and slip something in my ice water. I assumed that's what they would offer me since I look like I could use a glass.

I made my way towards the cottage. I've never wheeled this long before. My arms started to burn, but I tried to consider it a workout. Sweat pouring down my face with nothing to wipe it off with but my shirt. As much as I hated to do so, I did. No time to play pretty boy. As I approached the cottage I heard someone rattling around. I just didn't know where the noise was coming from.

"Who's there?" The voice says. It startled me and I dropped my phone in my lap. I finally answer. "Hi, I'm Alex. You don't know me, but I'm lost and need a little direction." I say. No answer. I still hear rattling noises but still not sure where it's coming from. I creep slowly over towards the old car. "Can you come out please; I'm a little freaked out right now." I say. More rattling.

"One second." He says. It sounded like the voice was coming from the car, but there was no one inside. Then I look under and see a pair of old dirty shoes sticking out from the back. "I can't seem to fix this stupid thing!" He yells as he rolls out from under the old car. As soon as his face came out from under the car my phone almost slipped out again. It was the creepy Asian guy from the plane. I noticed the tattoo on his face immediately. I just remember him staring us down because Venessa was snoring so loud. Out of all the people to help me it just had to be him. Looking around he seemed like my only option so I'd better be as nice as possible. He may not even help. He gave me that look as if he remembered me. "The young man from the plane, right?" he says. Oh great, now he remembers me.

I act as if my memory is a little fuzzy. "Umm... yeah, you were on there too right?" I say.

"I was. It was a long flight, and your little lady friend didn't make it any better with all that snoring." he says. I laugh as if it was a joke but his face was still motionless.

"Yeah we're still working on that. At least you don't have to room with her for a week." I say.

"I suppose that's a plus." He says. "So how did you manage to get way out here?" I can't tell a story without spurting out all the useless details to make the story more interesting, so I just give him the short version. Todd would be proud. "I wanted to take a drive. The stupid cab guy wasn't up for it so I told him to just let me out, and here I am." I say. I held back going into detail. It was harder than I thought.

"Stupid cab guy." He says sarcastically. Well at least he has a sense of humor. Killers don't have those, right? "So now you're stranded here out of the city and you need a ride back because you didn't think about that before, right?" Is this guy secretly giving me a lecture? Well secretly isn't quite the word. He just basically came out and said it. Gathering my thoughts trying to come back with something clever and with good reason behind it, I couldn't. There was no good reasoning behind it. A goat came from behind his yard. "So you're the goat guy. You know, you might be missing one, I saw another crossing the street about a mile and a half back that way." I say, pointing in the direction I just came from. I was mainly hoping the change of topic would shift the conversation.

"Yes she's mine. She'll be back. Goat guy? They are simply pets around here, much more easily to handle than a dog everyone keeps in their house." He says. One debate after another. It was too hot outside to banter about nothing. The sweat started to soak my shirt and I'm not use to having armpit stains.

"Can we go inside or something? We can finish our animal argument there... please?" I say. Not a good way to invite yourself inside someone's home, but the heat will make you say anything.

"Go inside? So you can kill me right?" he says with a chuckle.

"Well at least you know whose boss. I won't kill you if you don't slip anything in my water."

"Is that your way of saying you're thirsty? Because you can just ask if you need to wet your whistle." He says. Wow, we can go back and forth all day it seems like. I'm not sure if we are having friendly conversation or he's actually irritated that I interrupted him fixing his car. "Okay kid, let's take it inside. You can watch me pour the water." He says. We go inside and it was not like I had expected. Nice suede sofa, long velvet curtains, velvet table clothes, and a vase of flowers set by every window in the house. Not a place of a single man with goats who fixes cars all day. "You married?" I ask.

"Me? Nooo. Well not anymore. This was our place, but she packed up and moved on."

"Well, I'm sorry to hear that." I said.

"I'm not. Life is much better without the ranting of a crazy cynical woman all day. I can do what I please now."

"Yeah I would hate to see you two at it." I say laughing. He didn't laugh. I decided it was best not to joke anymore with this guy. My mission was to get back to the hotel before my phone died, and by the looks of it, I wasn't sure that was going to happen.

"Here is your poison free water."

"Thank you." I said. Another joke came to mind, but I refuse to fail at another attempt to make this man laugh. "So before we get any closer, do you want me to take you back to the city or not?" He asks. A little bit of an impolite way of putting it. It made me feel as if he didn't want to take me and if he didn't I didn't mind moving on to the next place to find someone who would. Then again, looking outside just made me sweat thinking about it.

"Yes, that would be great...if you can, that is. I notice your car isn't really going anywhere anytime soon." I say. "What you think I'm stranded here also. I have another car out back under that tarp. If you don't want to waste anymore of my time we can go now."

"Pushy, Pushy I thought for a second you were starting to like me," I said sarcastically. I guzzled down the last of the water and set the glass down on the table. We went back outside into the heat, and he unveiled another old car. "Are you sure this will get us there?" I say without thinking. That ungrateful comment could have just landed me a slow roll back home in my wheelchair.

"It gets the job done, that's all you need to know, but not without gas. We have to stop by the gas station on the way there if you don't mind the slight delay. Not that I care anyway." He said. Seems like I made a friend. He won't admit it, but he enjoys my company more than he knows. I'll just never hear him admit it. "Nope, don't mind at all." I say.

We pull up to the gas station and he gets out of the

car and walks into it. I see him arguing with the cashier then storms out heading back to the car. I rolled the window down to see what was the matter.

"Problem?" I ask.

"Yes, do you have change for a hundred? What gas station doesn't have change for a hundred?!" He yells.

"Umm...I'm guessing a gas station that gets no business?" I say. He knew I was making a small joke, and wasn't amused. Lucky for him and thanks to Tyler I did have change for a hundred. "Here are five twenties. Knock yourself out, and don't kill that poor lady while you're at it." I say. The jokes just kept coming around that guy. He brought the sarcasm out of me, and I seemed to be having too much fun with it. He hands me the hundred dollar bill.

"Thanks kid."

"Hey, don't mention it. Now we're even for you driving me back." I say. The drive didn't seem long at all. It could be the fact that he was speeding, and the cab driver was driving like a little old lady trying to run up the meter, or just obeying the law. We pulled up to the hotel and I never felt so relieved. Besides the moment Tyler showed up at the door with Venessa's purse. "Thanks a lot goat guy." I say. The whole time I didn't even know his name. That was awkward.

"No problem charity case".

"Well jokes aside, this charity case thanks you. You were a big help." I said.

"No problem. Just stay in the city limits next time. I would hate to see a kid in a wheel chair stranded on the side of the road... again." He says laughing. Oh so now he laughs. One of those guys that only laughs at his own jokes. Not as cool as he thinks it is.

CHAPTER THIRTEEN

I headed into the lobby and waved hello to the doorman, so glad to finally be back. I just wanted to lay in bed now with the vent blowing directly on me. Thinking about it made me move a little faster towards the elevator. My phone battery was on five percent. I made it there before it died. Mission accomplished. I opened the door to the room to find no Venessa. She was still out with Romeo. I wanted to be angry, but once I felt the cool breeze from the air conditioning I decide to go ahead and get ready to relax. I took everything out of my pants pockets which included my lucky rabbit's foot, a few quarters, and a couple of receipts, the hundred dollar bill, and my wallet. As I lay on the bed I set everything on the coffee table next to the bed, and as I started to put the hundred dollar bill into my wallet I noticed something. The bill had a smiley face on it, the same smiley face that Venessa puts on all of her bills. My eyes lit up. Could he have stolen her purse? Was it him all along? Without even thinking it all the way through I called Venessa, and she finally picked up. "Hey Alex!" She says in a cheerful voice. "Hey... umm, I have some news for you." I say.

After stumbling over my words trying to say too many things at once, Venessa interrupted me. "Slow down Alex, I'll be back in a few minutes." she says. "No, wait! I just need to-" I start. Then she hung up the phone before I could get the rest out. I sat wondering how goat guy ended up with the bill. Surely we didn't break a whole hundred on this trip yet, so it couldn't have gotten to him through purchase. I sit on the bed thinking awhile. Then soon my mind was made up. He had stolen it. Good news is he didn't know I knew yet, and I wondered if he even knew who he stole it from. Venessa took longer than expected and I worried a little. I called her phone but it went to voicemail. It must have died.

I lay back on the comforter with my feet dangling from the foot of the bed. I intended to just rest my eyes for a few minutes after a long day of sun, but ended up passing out in pure exhaustion. Venessa finally came through the door and shook me awake.

"Hey, Alex? Wake up." she says. My eyes opened. It just hit me that I had passed out. I look at my phone to see the time. It'd been an hour and a half since I called her.

"Where have you been? You said you'd be back in a few minutes!" I say loudly.

"Calm down! We went for ice cream after." she says.

"After what?" I asked.

"We were on a boat okay? It's no big deal I'm back now. Anyway, are you going to tell me what you were calling about earlier or not?" she says. I gathered my thoughts so my conversation didn't end up like the last. Then a flush from the bathroom sparked my attention. "Is he here?" I asked. "Yes, he picked up a movie we thought you'd like." Tyler comes out of the bathroom with a hand towel wiping his hands. "Hey buddy, guess what we got. *Remember the Titans!* Venessa said it was your favorite." he says. I couldn't be rude. It was a nice gesture. I wanted to continue on with what I discovered earlier, but it would just spoil the evening. Plus I didn't want to have this conversation in front of Tyler anyway.

"Thanks man, well let's pop that sucker in." I say. Venessa looks at me with her arms out as if our conversation wasn't finished. "Soooooo?" she says. "It's not that important after all. We'll talk about it later." I said. Tyler put the movie in and ordered some food. No matter how many times I've seen *Remember the Titans*, it never seems to get old for some reason. I can tell something was on Venessa's mind. It was my fault for letting the unknown lingers in her mind. In order to clear it I acted as if everything was fine. Joking with Tyler, then nudging her when a funny comment was said seemed to ease her mind. Tyler started to get tired. He yawned about seven times in a half hour, and kept looking down at his watch every few minutes. He was ready to go. I thought, any minute now he will stand up, look for his keys and say, "Well guys, that's it for me. I'll leave the rest of the movie for you two. Enjoy." That's what I imagined him saying at least. Saw this episode way too many times to be wrong. Venessa started to doze off herself, nodding back and forth into consciousness. Just about bedtime for everyone. I had a power nap so I was wide awake. Great, another night to spend gazing up at the ceiling thinking about my pathetic excuse for a life. Sure enough, fifteen minutes later Tyler started to get up, keys already in hand.

"Well guys I'm gonna head on. I have to get up early tomorrow." he says. Gosh I'm good. Not the exact way I pictured it, but close enough. Venessa gets up slowly. I can tell she was heading to bed right after he left, and lord knows I can't start a movie and not finish it so it looked like I'd spend the next hour watching it alone.

"Okay well thanks for everything today. I had fun." she says. She gives him a big hug. A hug that lasted longer than it should have in my opinion. Of course the jealousy kicked in, but managed to harness it once I'd gotten familiar with the situation. She walked him out leaving me to the movie. "I'll be right back." she says.

"Yeah yeah, that's what you always say." I mumbled under my breath. I was going to tell her, just not that night at least. I don't know why I was making such a big deal out of it to begin with. I mean, we got the purse back. Sure we didn't retrieve the money, but Tyler was nice enough to cover us for the rest of our trip without us having to call our parents to bail us out. That should have been enough to keep it quiet, but knowing me, it was going to come out one way or another. She would want to know right?

I peeked down out of the window to spy on the two. What was I looking for? A kiss maybe? That would crush me. For her to fall in love with a boy she just met rather than someone who's been by her side for years. I didn't feel good enough. These are the things I pondered while lying awake at night. Knowing that we had one full day left calmed me down. Nothing can come out of this fling anyway; he'll be forgotten in a week when we get back home. The night was a bit chill and the two were hugged up on the car with his back leaning against the passenger door. Not a sight I wanted to see. It seemed too romantic - as if something was actually happening between the two of them. No kiss. Thank God, no kiss. They hugged goodbye and she ran back up with her arms folded under her hoodie. I closed the curtains and got back to the movie. She knew me well enough to think I was spying on them. I didn't want any evidence of it left open when she walked in for it to even cross her mind.

"Still watching the movie?" she asked when she entered. "You know me. Can't finish it until it's over," I answered.

"Yeah, I guess that's accurate." she says. She hopped in her bed and lay down. I was still wide awake so going to bed before the movie went off was pointless considering I'd still be up all night. "I'm tired, so I'm just gonna go to sleep if that's okay with you." she says. No shock there. It's those little things that depress me. Just thinking about people bailing on me or skipping out so easily got to me. It could be just my low self-esteem talking. I never took myself too serious about the issues, but it didn't change the fact that it hurt inside. So I just say what I always say. "No it's cool" I say. No one ever knows what's bothering me. I keep it bottled up tight so no one will think I'm this pathetic little wimp in a wheel chair who feels sorry for himself all the time. When the movie went off, and I cut all the lights out I laid in my bed. Just laid there and thought - but is that who I am?

I woke up to see Venessa's bed empty, and already made. She was out on the balcony leaning over the rail overlooking the city. She turns around and has a glass in her hand.

"You finally up boy?" she says. "That better be grape juice in that glass!" I say. "Oh, you're not going to believe this. At our age, it's legal here!" she says jumping up and down, almost spilling the wine on the beige carpet. "How do you figure that?" I asked. "Well, I went downstairs to get us breakfast at the buffet, and saw a boy outside the window that looked younger than us drinking alcohol. I freaked out! Then told this guy that was hogging all the eggs in front of me that I can't believe the kid hasn't been caught by authorities yet. I mean, here he is walking around town with a bottle of wine, and no one is saying anything!" she said.

"Okay so what happened after that?" I say, trying to

hurry the story along.

"Well, the guy in front of me says, 'oh that kid? He's plenty old enough doll' and walks off laughing. Then I looked it up and it's true! Look it up for yourself!" she says in a loud voice.

"Oh, I believe you, and that's good for you because I'm not going to jail for anybody." I said jokingly.

"Oh is that right? Not even for me?" she asked. "Of course not. You see this pretty face? I can't risk anything happening to me behind bars, especially for someone who is in love with another guy." I said, still joking, but it got a bit awkward for a few seconds.

"Who are you talking about? Tyler?" I nod my head.

"I am not in love with him!" She shouts. "We are leaving tomorrow and even if I did we'll never see him again." The comment seemed to hit a nerve. "Alright, all right - defensive aren't we. It was a joke girl, calm down." I say. I was relieved she said that, but wasn't sure if she reacted this way because she did like him, or because she couldn't believe I would think such a thing.

The way they carried on proved to me that she liked

him a lot, but I wasn't going to say another word about it. "So when you found out, you went and got a bottle and decided to drink it this early? Have you ever had wine before? Oh and where is the breakfast that you went down there to get?"

"Whoa whoa now, slow down cowboy! Let me explain...geez. After standing in line I realized it would have been too cold by the time you woke up, so I didn't get any food either. Then when I realized we can drink, I figured on our last day here we can go wine tasting, but I had to try some before we go. You know, in case we hated it," she explained.

It sounded pretty logical to me. There was nothing I could be upset about.

"Well alright then." I said. I had nothing else to come back with, as always. "Last day! Let's make this one count."

"Agreed!"

"So does that mean just us?" I ask. She looks at me with that look she gives me when I say something, but have a larger meaning behind it.

"So what you're trying to say is, no Tyler, right?" she

says. Then after she figures me out, I act like I don't know what she's talking about. You know, the usual back and forth, but this mostly happens when you're married. Or so I've heard.

"Pshh, what? Whatever, I don't care about him. I mean I'm grateful for everything he did for us so why would I care if he came?" I say, hoping I sold it well.

"I don't know, why would you?" she says. The room got quiet for a second. This was a moment where Ross from

back home would usually pop out and shout: "AWKWARD!" Then do the awkward turtle move with his hands, making it even more awkward.

"Well, I don't care, but it's just obvious that this is my birthday trip, and I thought we'd spend it together. Not together, together but you know... friend together." I say. She takes another sip of her wine like she's been drinking for a while. "So how much have you had so far? You might need to slow down before we go out in public. This is your first time drinking you know. We have no idea what a drunken Venessa is like, and I'm afraid to find out." I suggest. She sets the glass down then takes another sip out of the bottle that she has been holding in her other hand the entire time. I can already tell today is not going to go as planned.

"Want some?" she offers.

"No thank you, I would hate to pass out in my wheel chair."

"Suit yourself boy scout. Well let's go! Let's get this day started." Thanks to Tyler we'd visited a lot of places so we were trying to figure out where to go to next after the wine tasting. Something I was not looking forward to, but who am I to say no to the secret love of my life.

I made a few phone calls back home, and everything seemed fine. Dr. Browden was doing his usual. Mom and dad were planning a trip of their own to Hawaii. I've never been myself and was always afraid to go, thinking if I did I may never want to come back. It's probably for the best.

CHAPTER FOURTEEN

I could barely even enjoy the ride due to my phone going off every second from Venessa's dad checking in, but checking in with the wrong person. I figure trying to get dirt on his daughter so he can catch her in a lie when she called. He's not going to get any answers from me. I've already failed him in one aspect. Nothing got serious, but I'm sure if we stayed another week or so she'd be headed to Vegas to elope, which I couldn't see myself let happen. Her dad trusted me a great deal. The fact that we got one room was enough. Then again it hurts my feelings in a way because that means he thinks I have no shot with her, and I'm thinking my disability plays a big rolling factor in that. I blocked it all out. One goal, and one mission, and that's to be normal. Don't treat me differently because you might underestimate me. That's how I see it.

I knew the wine tasting thing was a bad idea to begin with, but realized how much I didn't want to go when I didn't want to get out of the cab. "Let's go slow poke, we got some tastin' to do!" Venessa says. My body was a little sore but I didn't know why, and I wasn't going to make an excuse to Venessa about it because she knew I was not thrilled about going to begin with. She would only then think I was making exactly that, an excuse. So I sucked it up. The place looked like a castle on the outside, and on the inside it looked like we were in a classy cave surrounded by lights of different colors shining everywhere, purple, blue, and pink lights. There was an enormous table in the middle of the cave like structure, and wine bottles everywhere. Definitely nothing like this back home, and according to my facial expression Venessa was convinced I had changed my mind about not wanting to come. I did feel a little claustrophobic trying to get through. I kept on ramming people in the leg with my wheel chair.

Venessa kept apologizing for me because I was too embarrassed to say anything to anybody after tripping an elderly lady. When we finally got to sit down at the table, it got quite boring. "Hello everyone! My name is Joel De Smet! Sooo who's first time is it today?" he asked this guy was way too excited about tasting wine...or getting people drunk, one of the two. Who knew there was so much to tasting wine? I felt like we were in a wine education class, and perhaps we were. We had to look and observe the wine, swirl it in the glass to release violations... whatever that means. Then we had to sniff it, and when we finally got to taste it, once we took a sip the instructor told us to hold the wine in our mouths and suck air through it. I just looked at Venessa like, seriously, is this really necessary?

Every time we had to do something that seemed crazy to us I would glance in her direction and make a funny face. She was trying to be mature and listen to the instructor, following everything he said, but she couldn't keep a straight face much longer. She took another sip of the wine and attempted to suck air through it, but when I gave her a crazy look, she looked over my way and spit it all out with laughter to follow. The husband of an elderly lady that I tagged on the way in wasn't too mirthful about his wine tasting experience, especially since the majority of the wine Venessa spewed out sprayed all over his white linen shirt. Needless to say, we didn't stay much longer after that. I leaned over and whispered in Venessa's ear.

"Okay...what do you say we go get some ice cream?" I say. The smile on her face showed she liked that idea a lot, and we scooted out of there before they kicked us out. Despite the fact that we were in a cave, it was an exceptionally elegant cave. As much as we were both classy in our own way, we learned quickly that wasn't our scene. We realized how dark it was inside when we went outside and the sun hit us hard. "Whoa we should have brought our shades today! I didn't know why we didn't think of it!" Venessa says. I didn't know how I forgot mine. I could always count on a compliment from her when I had my aviators on. That always made my day, and the main reason I wore them. While we waited for a taxi, one finally pulled up, and was letting someone out.

"Hey that looks like..." I started and Venessa interrupted - "Oh, it is." The passenger gets out of the vehicle, and sure enough, it was Tyler. "Hey, what are you two doing here?" he asked. I should ask you the same question. Coming to get drunk by yourself?" Venessa asks jokingly.

"Umm no, actually I'm meeting a few friends here in a moment. I didn't take you for the type to drink. I hear they don't let you at your age in the U.S." he says.

"Well that's why we're doing it now, because it's legal. I guess that's why all of you are alcoholics here, because they start you off at a young age," she joked.

Tyler laughed. "By the way, why are you taking a taxi? Where's your fancy car?" I ask. "Well, my fancy car was in a wreck last night, along with me in it. I'm fine as you can tell, but my emotions are more damaged than the car. That's my baby."

"Well I'm sorry to hear that." Venessa stated solemnly. "Why didn't you call me? ... I mean us?" Adding the "I mean us" made me suspicious. Like she was trying to hide some type of secret relationship between the two, but his reaction proved otherwise.

"Well, I would have, but I wasn't hurt and it wasn't a

big deal so I didn't think about it. Didn't want to bring any extra drama to your vacation you know." Tyler said.

"Oh...well, understandable, I guess." she replied. An old blue Chevy pulls up. This car looks familiar, and I knew exactly who it was. I did not think I would see this guy again, but it seemed I was in for another sarcastic back and forth banter session with the Goat Guy. I wheeled back behind Venessa so maybe he wouldn't see me when he walked in, but he wasn't walking towards the door. He was walking towards Tyler. I hope they don't know each other, please God don't let them know each other, I thought to myself. I played it cool on the outside.

"Oh, here's one of them now." Tyler says. "What's up Tan? Where's the rest of the crew?" Tyler asks. Sure enough they knew each other, and obviously enough it was impossible to hide my wheel chair behind Venessa's small frame.

"Oh I just got off the phone with them, they are on the way." Tan answered. "Okay cool, well this is Venessa, the one who I've been telling you about, and this is Alex her good friend." Tyler says. "Well well, if it isn't charity case." Tan says. Tyler looks at me, and then looks at Tan.

"Wait, you two know each other?" he asked puzzled.

"Basically best friends as this point, or just some stranded stranger I helped out earlier this week that was lost. You pick." Tan said, laughing.

"Well if I knew you were coming I would have told you to bring your goats. Did the other one come back or just came to its senses and ran on away?" I asked.

"Umm what did I miss?" Venessa says. She looked so confused, and she was on the way of being upset with me because I didn't tell her about my little adventure. "Charity case didn't enlighten you? Well I wouldn't have either if I pissed the cab driver off and got stranded out in the middle of nowhere in a wheel chair. Good going sport." He was even more obnoxious around Tyler.

This could end badly if I don't come clean with the whole story, but I couldn't do it around Tyler, or Tan. After all it was their little evening together that sparked the whole idea in the first place. Coming across as the jealous friend wasn't going to make anything better, it would actually make it worse, plus crafting the idea in all of their minds that I had feelings for her, which would create an even bigger, not to mention a more awkward situation. Venessa still had that confused look on her face, and she wouldn't stop staring at me to hear my side of the story. I wouldn't look at her. I could just see her burning a hole through the side of my face as I saw her through my peripheral vision.

"I was going to tell you, but we both had so much going on at the time, and I made it back safe and sound so it wasn't a big deal." I explained.

"Yes thanks to me. I even invited him in for a drink, a non-alcoholic beverage that is, but it seems they drink after all." Tan says. Tan talking was just upsetting Venessa more and more. I hadn't even told her about the hundred dollar bill with the smiley face on it that he gave me to break for him at the gas station.

"What were you doing out so far? Tan doesn't even live in the city!" Tyler asks.

"Yeah Alex, what were you doing so far away?!"

Venessa adds with her hands on her hips. I just sat there with a million things going through my mind. I didn't know what to say, but whatever it was, I had to keep it short and simple until we got back to the house to talk it over.

"Look, it's my birthday trip; I can't venture out by myself if I want too? People get lost things happen, but I'm fine now and got the pleasure of meeting Mr. Charming Goat Guy over here. So can we drop it for now, please?" I ask.

Everyone just kind of looked around at each other nodding their heads in agreement, except for Venessa. She didn't ask any more questions right then, probably because she was planning on giving me the silent treatment all the way home. I just knew I was going to catch her fire as soon as we got back up to the room, so I was content with the silence for the short moment. As we arrive back to the hotel, she got out, slammed the door, and then headed up the steps by herself. She always helps me get my wheel chair out and pushes me up, whether I needed it or not. So I knew she was mad. The doorman felt pretty bad for me, and so like I did when I angrily left the cab out in goat country. I grabbed my chair and maneuvered it out and was sliding in it before the cabbie even got around to helping me. You get used to such things when you have to.

"Man what did you do to your lady friend brother?" he asks. "Long story, but you know how women are, always blowing things out of proportion." I said. He laughed then nodded his head. "Oh, I know what you mean brother, women these days are crazy. I'll have to tell you about my ex one of these days."

I didn't want to tell him it was my last day here because I didn't feel like hearing his story now, so I just told him we should hang sometime. You know, the thing people say and you know it's never going to happen, but you say it anyway to be kind. "Thanks again man for the help." I said.

"No problem, it's my job to help." he said, and I let it slide that I'd already helped myself before he'd hefted his weight out of the driver's seat anyway.

CHAPTER FIFTEEN

On the way up to the room I was rehearsing what I was going to say to Venessa. It had to come across smooth and understanding. I didn't want to make it seem like it was her fault, but if she was going to pin all the blame on me then I was going to have to call her out. As I opened the door, she was sipping on the wine, standing out on the balcony looking out.

"Drinking your sorrows away I see." I added a little chuckle at the end to lighten the mood. Didn't work! She turns around and sets the glass on the ledge and walks into the room. "So spill? Tell me what you were up to, wondering off outside the city without me." she said.

"I...I..." That's all I could get out right. How could I even start?

"You could have been hurt! Then what was I going to tell your parents?" she nearly shouts.

"I know it was dumb, but I was upset."

"Upset why?" she asked, still angry. Here it goes, I thought. I had to tell her everything or somehow come up with a lie. She could always tell when I'm lying. My heart started to beat fast. The same nervous feeling when I had to sing the national anthem at the JV basketball game in fifth grade.

"I was upset because it is my birthday trip, and you and lover boy were having your little romance and just left me out of the picture, that's why. I wasn't going to stay cooped up in the hotel all day, so I left. Is that so bad?" I say trying to match her tone of voice.

"So you're jealous? Is that it? Jealous of some guy I barely know that I'm never going to see again?" Her tone got higher.

"That's just it! Someone you barely know. Then here I am, someone who you do know and feeling like I don't even matter. We've been friends for so long and been through a lot, and you can't even see that....you can't even see..." I paused. My heart was pumping out of my chest, and I was shaking even more. I felt sick.

"See what?" she yelled.

"You can't see that I love you! There I said it! You couldn't see how much I loved you since the first time

I laid eyes on you!" I yelled back.

That feeling when something just comes out of you like word vomit, and you want to just grab it and stick it back in your mouth, that's what that feeling was like. We both sat there in silence for the next few seconds, with her mouth still wide open, although I'm not even sure she knew it was. Then I broke the silence, by changing the subject. "And I'll tell you something else! Tan, Tyler's friend traded me a hundred dollar bill for five twenty's that day, and do you know what it had on it? A smiley face! Can you tell me how that happened?" I asked loudly.

I calmed down for a second and took a couple of deep breathes to settle my heart rate. Her eyes widened. She still didn't know what to say. I hated how everything came out, but I guess there is no good time to tell your best friend you love her, and you found a bill of hers which the last time we saw was before her purse was stolen.

"I have to go." she said calmly.

"Go where?" I ask.

"I just have to go, and think about all of this, it's just

too much to handle right now, okay." she says.

"Oh just go, just go like you always do and leave me hanging."

She grabs her purse and heads out the door in a flash. What did I just do? I thought, before I crawled onto the bed and cried. I never cry, but it felt so good to. Letting out everything I felt while no one was there to see me wail was very therapeutic.

I cried for at least ten minutes straight, winey noises and all, just letting it all come out freely. I could have just ruined our friendship for good, and right then at that moment I know it would never be the same ever again. Things will get better, they just have to. My tears finally stopped. I felt a small peace come across me, and then I tucked myself under the covers after getting goose bumps when the air kicked back on. The air from the vent blew over my face making my wet cheeks even colder. Even with it being our last day in Europe, and the sun still peeking through the blinds, I fell sound asleep. My phone by my side, plugged into the charger, hoping for a call from Venessa.

You learn a lot when you take chances. Sacrifice is a big part of life, and growing up. So I'm told. I don't regret telling Venessa I loved her. It was killing me every day not to. I had slept peacefully through most of the evening, and it was around nine o'clock when I woke up. I looked around and Venessa was still not back. The next day at breakfast she didn't tell me where she went, and I wasn't going to ask. I assumed she was with Tyler. I hope she didn't tell him about everything I spilled yesterday, but I guess it didn't matter because we were leaving that day. We both were up all morning and barely said a few words to each other. I didn't know what to say. I was waiting on her to take the first step. I thought I'd taken all the steps I ever needed to take. Packing didn't take long for either of us. We basically kept the clothes in our suit cases to make it easier when we left. Our stomachs were satisfied and it was about time to leave for the airport.

I called Dr. Browden to see how he was doing. I felt like I hadn't talked to him all week, and I knew he wanted to make sure I'd be back in time for my check-up. I assured him I would be, and even though I had fun there, I missed Alabama in a weird way. Never thought I'd say that. I knew the doorman was going to miss us, he hugged Venessa and I real tight, and told us to come back soon. He was still wanting to tell me about his ex. Venessa looked at me like, what is he talking about, but I just nodded my head to him. "Alright man, when I come back you can tell me all about it." I said.

He was excited. He probably doesn't have many friends, or so it seems. We got in the cab and I still felt that awkward tension between the both of us. I knew she felt it too.

"You excited to go back?" I asked.

"Yeah, I am I guess. Never thought I'd say that." she says. Those were my thoughts exactly. The car ride was quiet. The palm of my hands started to get clammy. It was a nervous habit. A lot of people's nervous habit. I wanted to talk about it. I wanted to clear the air so we both were on the same page at least, no matter what the outcome. She started to mumble under her breathe.

"You say something?" I asked. "Um, No, well...no." she said with little confidence. "Well..." she pauses. Maybe this was it. It had to be killing her as much as it was killing me.

"Why did you say that last night?" she asked. Finally! She breaks. I jumped up and down on the inside, but on the outside I was stone. "Which part?" I ask. "You did say a lot, but the part when you said-" I interrupted her. "I loved you?"

"Yeah, I mean...is it true; or something?" she asked.

"Yes it is true, but I was out of line and I apologize. I meant every word, but if you don't feel the same then I understand." The cab driver glanced back and forth in his rearview mirror at us, just smiling. I didn't care if he heard everything. We had to settle this before we got back home. Even if we had to finish it on the plane, which looked like that's what we were going to have to do since we were a few minutes away.

"We can finish this later if you don't mind... but was there really one of my smiley faces on that hundred dollar bill?" she asked. I pulled it out of my wallet and handed it to her. "That's mine all right!" she says.

"How do you think he got it?"

"Well to be honest I thought he stole it. Think about it. We didn't purchase anything with a hundred dollar bill, in fact we converted only a little into Euros and you held on the rest. Yet that bill was in your purse before it was stolen. So my guess is, either he got it from the person that stole it, or it was him." I suggested.

She looks at me with a surprised face. "Wow! Well did you ask him where he got it?" she asked. "No I didn't want to jump the gun. He was helping me get back home ya know."

"Yeah that's true. The thief had to have seen my I.D. don't you think? I didn't see any reaction out of him when we saw him yesterday." I started to think for a second. I can't believe I didn't catch this before. I didn't want to blurt out conclusions on lover boy, but he was the one that miraculously found the purse. Turns out he is friends with Tan. What if he saw that Tan had stolen it and looked at the I.D. and realized it was us then returned it?

CHAPTER SIXTEEN

Venessa was looking out the window doing a little thinking of her own. I wonder if she sees the same pattern I do. It was stupid of me not to think of this before, but so much was going on in the middle of it all for me to even realize it.

"How did Tyler say he found the purse again?" she asked. She was thinking the same way I was. When all the drama died down, the pieces started to come together for the both of us.

"I don't remember. We weren't listening at the time, but I wish we were. Are you thinking the same thing I'm thinking?"

"I don't know, what are you thinking?" she asked.

"That Tyler is friends with Tan, and he just happens to find the purse. I don't know, maybe he saw that he had taken it, looked at the identification and saw it was yours and then returned it. Tan had already taken the money out of it, so he didn't need anything else out of it. Am I close?" I asked.

Her eyes got real big. "Wow, I guess we are on the

same page." The details were quite obvious. "Do you think we should call and ask him where he found it? Just tell him we forgot?" she asked. "Noooo, what good would that do? He gave the purse back, and the money is long gone. He felt bad enough for us as it is, and not to mention he gave us twice as much back out of his own pocket, so it worked out better for us. The guy's a saint; let's not bring it up at all." I said.

"Yeah you're right. What was I thinking? He did do a lot for us while we were here."

"Alright guys, you gonna get out or just run my meter up some more? Cause I don't mind if you do." The cab driver says. "Okay okay we're going, keep your shirt on old man." Venessa said.

"Seems like Europe put you on edge a little bit, huh?" I said jokingly. She hits me lightly on the arm and giggles. "Yep and you better not mess with me either."

The airport was packed. It's a good thing we arrived early because we wouldn't reach the counter for another forty minutes. Venessa started to dig around in her purse as we waited. "Hey Alex did we put the tickets in the suitcase?"

"No we left them in the purse remember?" I say. "Oh gosh." she says. "What?" I ask.

"I can't find them. I could have sworn they were just in here!" she says in a panic. "Okay don't worry. When was the last time you saw them?" "I don't know...I...I think I saw them in my purse yesterday when I went to pay for an Italian ice."

"When did you get an ice?" I ask. She stops looking through her purse for a moment, looks at me with her wide eyes.

"When I was with Tyler and Tan last night."

"Well call and ask him if he's seen them, maybe you left it in his car." I suggest feeling dread. "His car is in the shop, remember, we took Tan's car!" she says. What were we going to do now? Our plane would leave in a little over an hour and we didn't have our tickets, and couldn't afford to pay for new ones. I thought to call and ask Tyler for a loan, but that would be asking way too much. That's two thousand dollars! Even he might not have that kind of cash on hand to just give away. "So what do we do?" she asks. I brainstormed for a moment, but our options were limited. We didn't have a choice but to call Tyler to see if he could check Tan's car, or maybe back track where they had been last night. We couldn't leave, not now. We would definitely miss our flight, and even if Tyler agreed to search for the tickets, he wouldn't make it in time.

Venessa sat down on one of the waiting chairs. "We're dead! Our parents are going to kill us!" she says. Normally I would try to cheer her up by saying they didn't have to know, but if we didn't show up back in the states, they clearly would. "Okay, so is calling our parents out of the question?" I asked.

"Definitely! Don't you dare call them! At all!" she says in a threatening voice. "So what do we do then, huh? I mean, if we miss our flight, my parents will kill me even more because I won't be back in time for my checkup. Actually they might not have to kill me; I might die before we get back."

"Why is it such a big deal to have your check up every week? I don't get how it's that serious. You look fine to me. Stop worrying so much." she said.

"Me worry? You're the worrier! I don't know why it's so important okay; I just know that it is to my parents and doctor. That's all that matters to me." I say. "Well let's stop talking and do something, quick!" she says. Time was running out. We now had fifteen minutes to board the plane or we were going to be left there. Venessa called Tyler five times within three minutes. We got no answer. We were officially wrecked.

We both sat there thinking of what we were going to do next. The only thing left in my mind was to call our parents and tell them we messed up and lost the tickets. We were lucky enough they didn't find out about the purse. Maybe we're not as responsible as we thought we were. Not to point fingers here, but if you wanted to get technical, Venessa is the irresponsible one, in both cases. "Our parents are going to find out sooner or later, so why don't we just come clean now?" I asked. "No! Not yet!" she yelled. I could tell she was one of those use to getting into mischief. Her parents probably let her go with me to test her responsibility. So she couldn't ask her parents for help. Then she would have lost. Time was winding down before the gate closed. My heart was pounding fast. I didn't want to stay any longer. It was time for us to go home, but that wasn't going to happen today. "How much money do we have combined?" she asks. "I have one hundred and thirty four dollars left." I say. "Okay, I have two hundred. Thank you Tyler!" she says kissing her dollar bills. "So what's the plan?" I asked.

She immediately runs towards the door, "come on!" She yells. I wheeled as fast as I could, trailing behind her. She waves for a cab, but as she sees one pulling up for someone else she runs in front of the woman and gets in. "Hurry!" She says. I could only go so fast and felt sorry for the person who had been waiting for that cab. She wasn't too happy about it, and the death stare with the middle finger raised made that clear. I stumbled into the cab and banged my elbow on the side of the door. The pain was intense for the first ten seconds then started to fade away. "Where are we going?" I asked.

She tells the cab driver an address I was not familiar with. She looks at me still panting hard from running.

"It's Tyler's house. We need help, and can't go to our parents just yet. So I have a plan." She said. She didn't have a plan. Not a full plan at least. I called her bluff, but I figured we had nothing else to lose. "There it is on the right!" Venessa tells the cab driver, as if he couldn't read directions.

We get out and Venessa rushed to the door and left me to fend for myself. I've done everything you could possibly do in a wheelchair by myself many of times, but she spoiled me on this trip by being at my side at every moment. The annoying sound of Tyler's doorbell startled me, and it didn't help that Venessa held the button down to drag the noise out. Tyler answered immediately.

"Hey I just got your message! I was about to call you! I'm so sorry you missed your flight, come on in." He says. My elbow was still throbbing a bit. I ignored the pain since that was the least of my worries. If I didn't get back in time for my shot, my parents would freak, and Dr. Browden might have a heart attack. "Well make yourself at home guys, there drinks in the fridge. I have to go to the bathroom so I'll be right out. Then we'll talk about everything." Tyler said. What would we do without Tyler? He'd been there since day one, and whenever we seem to screw up, he bailed us out. I personally felt bad that he had to. We should have just called our parents and confessed, but Venessa would never forgive me if I called. So I had to suck it up.

CHAPTER SEVENTEEN

I started to massage my elbow and as I did I saw blood seeping through my white long sleeve shirt. "Oh my goodness Alex, are you okay?" Venessa asked.

"I'm fine."

She doesn't like the sight of blood. She could also see it in my eyes that I was in pain. "We need to get a band aid on that quick!" she said. Tyler's bag was sitting on the couch next us. I remember the last time we all hung out, Venessa pricked her finger on a rose, and Tyler grabbed his travel first aid kit out of his bag and attended to her. I'm sure the same visual was going through Venessa's mind because she reached over me to grab it. She fumbles through the bag, "I bet it's still in here." She says. Slowing down her search then coming to a complete stop, her eyes got wide. Her face became pale within seconds, and her mouth was wide open. I said nothing because I was still focused on the wrecked expression on her face. I gave her a second. She then looks at me as her eyes slowly dim back to normal, then pulls out something familiar. The tickets. I felt my heart skip a beat. Why on earth would he have the tickets? It just didn't make sense. Maybe he forgot they were in his bag. We both hear the toilet flush.

Venessa gets up from the couch as Tyler walks out of the bathroom. "Venessa wait." I say following her. "What is this?" Venessa screams, flashing the tickets in his face. "Whoa whoa calm down." he says. "I can explain." Venessa throws her hands over her hip then starts to breathe heavily. She actually seemed ready to hear him out. It just didn't make sense for him to do something like this. He'd been our guardian angel the whole time so the least we could do was see what he had to say first before we attacked him. I wheeled my way next to her. Tyler starts to walk over to his dining room table. Very elegant table clothes, shiny silverware, and a beautiful vase placed in the center with roses stemming from it. We followed slowly. He brushes his hand lightly over the top the roses. "You know Venessa...These were actually meant for you." he said. He was acting strange. A Tyler that seemed a bit different. Same appearance, but a sense of evil in his eyes. He picked the vase up. Then he sniffed the flowers.

"Alex...or should I say Stephen, I've been waiting for you to wake up... and smell the roses." He said. "Stephen? Who's Stephen?" I asked. We started to back up slowly. Tyler didn't appear to be in the right state of mind at the moment. Or was he ever?

"Oh...so I guess you haven't wakened up yet, have you?" he says. Venessa and I looked at each other, more confused than we ever have been.

I didn't know what to say back. Venessa kept running her fingers through her bangs. Her nervous habit I picked up on the first time we met, and the first time we fought. I myself was moving my wheelchair back and forth in fear. Our eyes locked for about five seconds, and as I turned my face towards Tyler to speak, he swings and shatters the vase over my head, knocking me out of my chair. My body started to twitch in a motion as if I was having a seizure taking my mind off the pain in my elbow. My vision became blurry. Venessa screamed loudly, and then jumped on

Tyler's back. He swung her around trying to sling her off, but her grip was too tight around him. Her arm locked under his neck blocking his airway. He could barely breathe, which brought him to his knees with her still behind him. There were broken pieces of vase everywhere, and a small sharp piece was digging through Tyler's cheek as Venessa pinned him down on the ground with her arms still wrapped tight around his neck, not letting up.

Was she going to kill him? She had more strength then what I imagined. Out of nowhere Tan comes from the back room. He grabs Venessa's hair, yanks her off of Tyler, slinging her into the dining room table as her head connected with the cedar. If only I could help her. I was defenseless. My body felt like it had turned into a vegetable. Now, not only could my lower body not move...neither could my upper. I couldn't even crawl. Venessa was still down, motionless. Tears flowed down my face immediately. If he killed her, I knew I would never be the same again if - I live through it. I had to get to her to check her pulse. I waited until my vision came back just enough. The feeling in my upper body came back enough for me to make one last move. Tyler and Tan were nowhere in sight from what I could see. Putting every ounce of strength I had left in me, I reached my arm out grabbing onto the carpet, and slid as hard as I could on my stomach. Not enough to get to her just yet. My body was telling me I couldn't move anymore but my mind was telling me I had one more push in me. I flailed my arm in front of me once more, giving it another push. *I can do this*.

My body finally started to move. My stomach sliding slowly along the carpet, and as I reached her, I looked up. A boot came towards my face knocking me in the head, but leaving me still conscious. I kept my eyes closed. They stung in the attempt to open them, and swelled up instantly. My mind gave up fighting and my body surrendered as I passed out on the floor next to Venessa.

CHAPTER EIGHTEEN

I'm not sure how long we were out, but when I came to, I opened my eyes to an empty room. No bed, no desk, no nothing - just a window that was boarded up with plywood. A stream of light poured in through the cracks. The light was bright. It must be the next day I thought groggily. The sun had started to go down a bit when we reached his house after leaving the airport. We were both in wooden chairs tied up from behind with clothe tied around us that smelled like Tyler's cologne. Maybe a ripped sleeve from one of his t-shirts. Our arms were tied tightly as well as our mouths and legs.

The room seemed quite new from what I could tell. The same carpet in the living room was in this room. So we had to still be in the house. Blood was dripping from the side of my head onto my jeans. Still I felt nothing but a huge headache. My vision was better, but the dizziness swayed it a bit. Venessa still had her head down. Either she was sleeping or still unconscious. I tried to call out to her, but nothing but a light mumbling noise came out. At least I know she's alive, I thought. If we make it through this I promised myself I would definitely never let her go. Her lying on the floor left me knowing one thing. That it wasn't just a high school crush. I really loved her. Tied behind her back, her hands started to twitch and she woke up in a panic and looked around noticing everything I had realized when I awoke. We were kidnapped. I wanted to know what she was thinking but I think I had a clue.

Where are we? What was going to happen to us? At least that's what I was thinking. What Tyler said the day before stuck in my head, talking about smelling the roses, and calling me by a different name. It just didn't make any sense to me. I tried to break my wrist free but it wouldn't budge. It was apparent I was still weak from the day prior. I needed nourishment. We hadn't eaten since the day before, and I knew how sick Venessa got when she hadn't eaten. There had to be a way out. From the looks of things the attempt to escape was not within our grasp. I could see Venessa struggling to break free as well. Her wrists were dark red. Her skin was starting to rub raw, and a panic attack was forming. If I could see mine I would say it looked about the same. It felt the same. Our parents are probably worried sick. I could only imagine what could be going through their minds. The door opened slowly. It was Tyler. Venessa stopped fidgeting with the rope. He didn't have food in his hands which irritated me. You would think knocking us unconscious and then locking us in an empty room tied up would raise some questions. Which of course it had, but neither of us could think with our stomachs in knots.

"How are you doing without your medication Alex? Anything yet?" He asked. It appeared that he knew about my medical history, and that freaked me out. He left me no choice not to answer anyway with his cloth snug around my mouth. I tried anyway, but he couldn't make any of it.

"What was that?" He asked. He removed the cloth from my mouth to let me speak. My mouth was almost completely dry from lack of substance, but I gathered up enough saliva swishing it around in my mouth. As he came closer, I hawked everything I had saved up into his face. I flinched and quickly shut my eyes as he bald up his fist and swung towards me knocking me in my jaw. My chair wobbled as I struggled to stay balanced, but failed as Tyler kicked the chair. I heard Venessa's stifled scream as I felt myself going down and there was nothing I could do about it. As I hit the ground a sharp pain seized my head. Liquid was dripping from my lips as I coughed making my mouth water up, but it wasn't saliva. It was blood.

My mind flashed into a room, and there I was, demonic. My eyes were the color of evil and I sat in a white padded room beating on the walls until my hands were numb screaming at the top of my lungs. I came to, and as I opened my eyes and saw that I remained on the floor with my face in my own blood and Tyler knelt down speaking but sounding muffled due to my head trauma. His voice slowly eased into my ears like a volume button being turned up.

Anything yet?" He asked again. I lay there my body throbbed. I sucked all the moisture I could into my mouth. Venessa sat there trying with all her might to free herself from the rope.

"I didn't think so. Well I'll come back when you do." Tyler said. He picked the chair up and put me back in it, along with the rag back in my mouth. He wiped his face of the spit I spewed in his face and slammed the door behind him. I tried to think about what he was talking about but I had nothing. Him calling me Stephen still lingered in my head, and it bothered me. Venessa stopped struggling, and just looked me in my eyes. She didn't even try to mumble anything. Instead she scooted closer and closer to me in her chair without falling over, then rested her head on my shoulder.

We sat there staring at the boarded up window watching the sun go down through the tiny cracks. She had fallen asleep on my arm. The discomfort of being unable to move because I might wake her didn't bother me. I laid my head softly on Venessa's head and finally drifting off to sleep as the pulsating pain in my head drifted away slowly.

It was such a vivid dream.

A man and his wife so madly in love. I can tell because he wouldn't let her out of his sight. She went to open the oven to check on the food and he came up and grabbed her from behind, wrapping his arms around her waist then kissing her neck. The grin on her face was enormous. I can smell the roast lingering in the air. "Hey, do you love me?" The man asked. She turns around and looks into his eyes. "You know I do." she says. He brushes his hand across her forehead, moving the bangs from her eyes. "I thought you might." He says with a smile. She laughed and threw a piece of broccoli at his chest. The chemistry between the couple was strong. It was a love I had never seen before even in my own parents. There was a knock at the door, a hard knock. The woman went to open it, and as she took a step the man grabbed her arm and pulled her back into his arms. "Just one more kiss." He says. She grins. "You're such a sap, you know that?" She says. As he hugs her he sees someone with a black mask on peeking through the window. As he makes eye contact with the stranger, the drifter removes his mask so his face is shown and looks him dead in his eyes. The man clenches her tighter. The face he saw must have been a familiar face seeing that his pleasant smile dropped immediately. The outlander put back on his mask and disappeared from the window as soon as she turned around. "We have to go." He whispers to her. "Is it them?" She asked. "Yes it is, but we have to stay calm...follow me." He says.

They duck low and crawled upstairs so the clamping of their footsteps would not be heard. They started to pack immediately, throwing everything they had into their suitcases. The knocking on the door continued. It got louder every time. The couple remained calm, but you can tell there was an enormous amount of fear in their eyes. "He is still sleeping Ben. We have to wake him up." She says in a panic. He opens up the window to the bedroom. "You go. You go first and I'll catch up I promise. I put our tickets and passport in your suitcase so you have everything. Just go we'll be fine...I promise." He says. Tears flowed down her face instantly. He grid his teeth, and held back his tears to be strong for the both of them. His jaw muscles poked out of his cheeks showing his restraint. A loud banging noise came from downstairs. She looks at Ben shaking. "Are you sure?" "Yes go!" He yells. They were coming. Whoever was coming wasn't here for a pleasant visit. The noise happened again, as if someone was trying to break down the door. A thunderous noise echoed throughout the house, and you can hear footsteps screeching on the wooden floor below.

Whoever was still sleeping was sure to be wakening up by now. Two incomers dressed in black charged upstairs. Ben heard them coming. He took off his shoes to lessen the noise of his footsteps on the floor, and then sprinted down the hall to another room. He opened the door to a room filled with action figures, and a Spiderman bed-set. Yet no one was in it. The intruders were close, tip-toeing around the hallway. Ben never called out the boy's name. He just quietly looked around the room. Ben could feel them coming towards the master bedroom. He hoped his wife had listened and gone when he had told her too, but he knows her all too well. She wasn't going to leave her child, but in the back of his mind he wanted to believe she escaped. Maybe she had hidden herself well. There was a secret door in the room that was inside the closet. It would be difficult to find even for a professional. Ben slowly opened the bathroom door that was connected to the room, and stood inside the tub with his child's baseball bat in his hand. Just waiting for their arrival. He hears a loud scream. Her voice. It was her voice screaming from the top of her lungs. She hadn't left as he expected, but still didn't want to believe it. They dragged her into the hallway and burst into their child's room. Ben stood steady with bat in hand, trying not to weep out loud. Then I awoke. Strangely, my mouth gag and Venessa's were gone. Tyler must have removed them while we were sleeping. Maybe he was afraid the hunger fumes with no path to escape would choke us to death before he could.

Once again sweat pouring down my face, and my t-shirt soaked. A feeling I had once before. I thought back to the last time this happened to me, and as I remember correctly it was the time we had just moved to Alabama. Dr. Browden wasn't able to give me my shot so I had to wait until he sent it in the mail, but I went a day or two after the time I was supposed to receive it and had a crazy dream that night. It was around the same length of time after I was supposed to get my check up so this has to be some sort of side effect. Hallucinations maybe? I'd had a couple instances where I've sweated profusely. What did this mean? I may have missed a day at best, but it never affected me as much. Must be the added stress, I thought.

CHAPTER NINETEEN

I sat there confused trying to piece everything together but I had nothing. My body was feeling weak, but then again that could be from lack of food. I wondered how my family is doing, they couldn't be doing well. My absence two days after I was supposed to be home had to be killing them. Venessa was still asleep. I wanted to wake her to talk, but being asleep not thinking about food when your stomach is touching your back is not such a bad feeling under the circumstances. So I waited. I couldn't sleep the rest of the night. The chair was torturing me and I would give anything to just lie down in a normal position. Even if I was still tied up. I had no watch to tell what time it was, but judging from outside through the tiny cracks I figured it to be around three in the morning. Why was this happening to me? I kept thinking if I had chosen another place to vacation would any of this have occurred. Only time will tell.

I closed my eyes real tight in hopes to fall asleep again, something to take my mind off of eating. I managed to sit there on auto pilot. Not all the way asleep, but not all the way awake either. Venessa had a good rest. Because of how small she was, she was able to position herself in the perfect angle to fall asleep in the uncomfortable wooden chair. My eyes were squinting a bit. I had drooled on myself the remainder of the early morning. Some of it had dried up on my chin. The air condition cut on, and I immediately smelled bacon flowing through the vent. Just the scent of it was good enough for me. Or perhaps it just makes the craving worse? Venessa was still sleeping. It was safe to wake her up at this point. She had a full nights rest as far as I was concerned.

"Venessa...Venessa." I said quietly. She finally picks her head up, yawning big enough to where I could see her uvula. "Do you smell that?" I asked. "Still trying to fully comprehend what was going on, she sits up from her slouched position. "It's food! It's breakfast!" She says loudly. "Shhhh...We don't exactly know it's for us yet. He hasn't exactly been a hospitable host ya know." I said. The door opened slowly. Tan stuck his head through the door suspiciously. He opens it fully, and walks in with two plates covered with paper towels. My mouth watered as the aroma thickened. It was for us.

We finally get to eat. It's crazy how we appreciate the small things when we are in a certain situation. Being tied up, locked in a room with nowhere to go, no one to talk to but each other.

"Don't talk. He wasn't going to cook for you at all. He laid a pop tart on the table for you two to split, but I couldn't let you starve like that." Tan says.

Venessa rolls her eyes. "You can help us a lot more by letting us out of here. We haven't done anything to you to deserve this." She says.

"You're correct. You haven't done anything to ME." He says. The statement was clear enough. We or I had done something to Tyler to make him retaliate this way. What could I have done that was bad enough for him to kidnap us and starve us to death? No thoughts had crossed my mind at the moment, but my mind was mainly on the freshly cooked bacon sitting before us. Venessa and I forgot our table manners completely. We inhaled the food, some bites without chewing. "Hurry and eat up, then give me your plates.

I don't want him to know I did this." Tan says.

The revving of a motorcycle engine sounded in the distance. I estimated a couple blocks away, maybe closer. Tan's eyes grew wide. "He wasn't expected back for another hour, what is he doing back so soon?" His hands were shaking, and he straight off grabbed the plates from each of us as Venessa reached out to take her last bite of eggs. He tried to play it cool seeming that Tyler was supposed to be his buddy. He didn't want to come off scared and weak. He knew more. He knew what Tyler was planning, and from the frightened look in Tan's eyes I could tell whatever it was, it wasn't going to be pretty. The noise became louder. Tan rushed downstairs to dispose of the plates he had given us for breakfast, and the smell of bacon still lingering in the air. Our stomachs were finally satisfied at the moment, but the thought of missing a meal tomorrow had crossed our minds if Tan was caught.

I heard the motorcycle come around the corner but it was impossible to see who it was through the cracks. I guess we knew it was Tyler all along, but trying to stay unafraid, there was always a slight chance in our minds that it was someone else. Every time I closed my eyes I could see my fate. Tyler's motives were unclear at that time, and there was no prediction of what would happen to us next. So there was nothing left to do but listen. We heard everything. We heard keys rattling, we heard whispers, and we knew when they went to sleep and when they woke up. We kind of developed a wolf like sense of hearing, and a new craving of paranoia. Being detained was one thing, being crippled was another. How could I run if I was chased, and how could I defend myself when the opportunity presented itself? These are the things that went through my mind every day for those days, and wanting nothing but to be strong, it only drove me crazy.

"What are you thinking about over there?" Venessa asked curiously. "Just thinking, I guess…not much else to do ya know." I say.

"Yeah you're right. I never thought I'd say this, but I miss home…like a lot."

I laughed a little. "Yeah don't we all? If we make it

out of here I don't think I'll ever argue with my brothers again." I say. "Oh don't say that. We will make it out of here, and let's be honest, you will argue with your brothers. Probably the day you get back." She says.

Tyler opened the door quickly. I didn't even hear him walk up the steps. "So how goes it?" He says energetically, as if we were put up in a grand hotel with room service. "This is torture man you can at least feed us?" I say loudly.

"Feed you? As far as I'm concerned you don't deserve to eat. Then again it appears you two have had a hearty breakfast this morning anyway." Tyler said. Venessa and I looked at each other. She wiped her mouth with her shoulder thinking evidence was shown on her face.

"Oh, I hope you don't think I'm stupid, but don't worry I took care of the contributor." He said.

"What did you do to him?!" Venessa yelled.

"Oh now you care about him after he gives you a couple pieces of bacon. Let's not forget he was the one who informed me you two were on the flight to

Europe. Let's not forget he was the one who came up with the idea to steal your purse in order for me to get on your good side. Oh…wait, you didn't know that did you?"

Venessa and I both sat there in silence and in complete shock. "We know all about you Alex, and you too Venessa. This was planned before you even decided to take your little birthday trip. I'm just sorry the love of your life here had to endure the pain with you. I couldn't just let one of you go." He said.

I tried to speak, but words just wouldn't come out of my mouth. I kept opening and closing it hoping to say something meaningful, but I was too disturbed. How could I not have known any of this? "Oh, and just one more thing. You are lucky to be alive Alex" Tyler added.

"Is that so?" I muttered.

"Why yes it is so."

"How do you figure that?" I ask. "Just ask your new buddy Tan who you two all of a sudden seem quite fond of. Let's just not take away from the fact that I am the victim here. You owe me everything. Sleep tight." He said as he walked backwards until he got to the door with a huge grin on his face, and then slammed it behind him.

"How could he do this?!" Venessa yells. She started to cry instantly. Before thinking we were going to make it out alive, now she wasn't so sure. If this had been planned and well thought out from the beginning, they must be taking it seriously. The crazy part about this entire thing is that we had no earthly idea what IT was. I couldn't think about what it was anymore. Thinking just made me sick. There was more thinking to do though, and that was how to get out of there. I was drained from the information I heard alone, so scheming our way out of there would have to wait for now. As if we had time.

Venessa managed her way over to poke her head through the biggest crack available at the window to see what was going on outside. Just daily life going on as normal with no idea what was going on in that house. Screaming for help wouldn't do much good, it would just make Tyler more upset and he would punish us by probably withholding the pop tart he was thinking about giving us. There was a soul inside him somewhere, but I didn't think it would ever show being that his intent for keeping us there was stronger. Venessa stared through the window for hours. I didn't talk much. She seemed to be in deep thought as I was earlier. No telling what she was pondering, so I didn't want to disturb her. Each time I went to talk I bit my tongue.

CHAPTER TWENTY

Each hour I tried to loosen the rope tied behind my back. The knot was extremely complicated as if he had done this before. They did appear looser than before since they were cutting off my circulation the first day. The sores on my wrist still hadn't healed from me trying for hours to break free the first day. I tried every chance I got. I never really thought about what would happen if I actually did. Nothing would happen. I would remain there. My wheelchair was downstairs with Tyler and Tan probably in the same spot I was in when I crawled over to Venessa to check if she was still breathing. Venessa ended up falling asleep against the window. She seemed at peace. She struggled with her rope just as much as I did the first day, but I saw that she had stopped trying. Had she given up completely?

Had she lost hope? There was a subtle knock at the door. Who would knock on the door? It was very light, and Venessa, as hard as she sleeps woke up and peered towards the door. In our minds it was someone other than Tyler or Tan. Maybe it was someone here to save us. Then the most unexpected person opens the door. It was Tan. My heart sank and our optimism was lost. After all I'd heard he was the last person I wanted to see, even more than Tyler. He walked in the room and his face had bandages on it with bruises peeking out from the sides. The repercussions of giving us breakfast I suppose. I had no sympathy.

"So you decided to be courteous and knock first? What did you think we might have been changing, and you wanted to make sure we were decent? Oh wait we can't change because we're tied to a freakin chair!" I say aggravated.

"I know you're upset, and I get it, but you have to understand in the beginning I only heard one side of the story." He says calmly.

"What story!" I screamed. "There is no story! We were just living our lives as normal just like everyone else until you two came along. What story are you idiots talking about?!" I yelled.

"Alex calm down." Venessa says.

"I'm not going to calm down. You heard what he did to us!" I yelled in rage. Tan walks closer towards the edge of my chair. "You take another step and I'll spit in your ugly face." I say.

"Yea he'll do it too." Venessa added.

"Listen, I can't tell you what we know. Tyler wants it to come out a different way. I just came here to apologize and let you know that Tyler is planning on killing you both after this is all over." He says.

"What! Venessa says in a teary voice. "Don't worry just yet. I have a plan to help you get out, but I need you to help me." He said.

"Help you? Why would I want to help you?" I asked.
"

"The help isn't really helping me, it's helping you. You have to remember. You just have to remember what happened that night, and this will all be over." He says.

"Remember what?" I asked.

"Just remember. You'll understand later." Tan said.

"No. I don't have to remember anything because we're going to die anyway. You don't care about us and, I don't trust you with anything." I say.

"So what about you Venessa? Can you trust me?" He asked.

"No. I stand by Alex…We have done nothing wrong and this is unforgivable." She says. I nod my head.

Tan walks over to the window where Venessa is sitting. "Pretty isn't it? Do you really want to wonder what if when your life flashes before your eyes? I understand what you're going through." He said.

"No you don't! You don't understand anything we're going through." She whimpered. Then she started to cry. I wanted to hold her so bad, but I couldn't make my way over there.

"According to Tyler, I'm lucky to be alive. What was he talking about?" I say.

"I don't know what you're talking about." Tan said nervously."

"Don't be a coward! What did he mean by that?" Venessa says sternly.

"If you want us to trust you, you'd tell us." I said. The room was calm. Tan sat Indian style on the floor, and sighed.

"Do you remember when you had that fall out in class? When you couldn't stop sweating and your body became numb?" He asked.

"Yeah, how did you know about that? We never told anyone here about that." Venessa says.

"Well that was…that was me."

"What how?" I asked.

"Listen I was trying to help you. I thought that if I could help you remember what you did then you wouldn't have to go through any of this. All Tyler wanted was for you to remember, and apologize. Then later on his rage got the best of him." He explained.

"I don't understand." I said, confused.

"I was serving lunch that day at your school. It was set up. I put something in your food that I thought would trigger your brain away from the…you know what I've said too much already. The bottom line is I'm not the guy that Tyler's making me out to be. Things are complicated with us, and I had no choice but to help him." He says. "So you put my life at risk?" I asked.

"I didn't know you would react that way to the medicine, I really didn't. I thought it would work, but it must have needed something else. I never figured it out. It'll all be clear to you later, but for now you'll just have to believe me." He said.

"Do you know I almost died that day? Do you not realize I know what harm that did to my body? I saw it in my doctor's eyes when he picked up the clipboard." I said.

"Oh, and that's another thing..." Tan starts then stops.

"What are you talking about now?" I asked.

"The day he collapsed outside his house...That was you too?!" Venessa yelled.

"Yeah but it's not what you think!" He yelled back defending himself."

"What I think is that you go around poisoning people you know nothing about." I stated. Tan stands up.

"Oh I know you and your family more than you know, especially Dr. Browden." He said. "What I did was for your own good, and you'll thank me later." He added.

"Get out of here! Leave now!" I scream. Tan walked

around my chair.

"Have you been having dreams Alex? Not normal dreams, but dreams that come to life like you never seen before?" Tan asked.

"What is he talking about Alex?" Venessa said.

"It's nothing."

"Nothing? It's a lot more than nothing I assure you. These dreams you're having have everything to do with this situation. Soon you will realize that. Now you two don't forget about what we've talked about today. It's very vital you stay focused." Tan walks over to the closet.

He reaches inside and grabs an old red tool box out. He reaches for the hammer tossing it back and forth in his hands, and walks towards Venessa. Her eyes locked on the tool anticipating his every move. He takes the back end of the hammer and pry's off a nail from one of the ply wood nailed to the wall blocking the window. He moves it up a few inches. We both squint as the sun beams in brighter than it had before. Then he nails it back into the wall. "I thought you might appreciate a little more sunlight. It seems a bit depressing in here." He winked, then packs the hammer back in the tool box and sets it back in the closet. Then he walked towards the door. He tilts his head down and as he grabs the door handle he turns around. Then he picks his head back up. "I'm sorry you guys are going through this. I know it must be hard and confusing. Just remember. Remember it all." Then he walked out the door.

CHAPTER TWENTY-ONE

We both sat there in silence not really knowing what to say. We hadn't spoken much the past couple days because we're both still in a stage of shock and our bodies were weary. Still registering everything and taking it all in I supposed. The word "remember" stuck in my head like it was something I was told before. After pondering for a bit I came to realize it was the note. The note that was left on the doorstep of the hotel the night Venessa didn't come home. It was him, it had to be him. Maybe he was trying to warn me, or even threaten me. I didn't know what to think at this point, but the pieces haven't come together just yet.

"So about those dreams…You really do know what he's talking about don't you? You can tell me you know." Venessa said.

"I keep on being told to remember, and yes I do see things in my dreams, and it feels like I'm really there. I can't explain it. I could just feel and smell everything around me, it's weird. The thing is I don't know what they mean. So if this is the reason we are here, I haven't figured out the connection." I explain.

"Well don't be afraid to talk to me okay. We are in this together." She says. I can't worry about anything else but that now. That was our ticket out of here. The crazy dreams I was having had to be telling me something, but what? Venessa scooted back over towards me, and laid her head on my shoulder. That was her hint that she didn't want to talk anymore, just sleep. I rested my head on hers, and once again watching the sunset drop slowly as we dozed off to sleep. There was no care anymore. There was no worry. There was just right here, and right now. The time we spend together is all we have, I thought, and I wouldn't want to be trapped in a room with anyone else. I can honestly say I was thankful for that.

My eyes twitched as I was drowned in a deep dream that led me to a dark room. This time it seemed like a nightmare. The two intruders slowly crept into a small room, both with a 9mm pistol silencer. Trying not to make a sound, one of them accidentally stepped on a power ranger. You couldn't hear a pen drop so the sound of an action figure being crushed by a steal toed boot made a great deal of noise. Ben was standing behind the bathroom curtain with no fire arm, just a bat. He was barefoot, and his feet were cold from the fiberglass tub he was standing in that was still wet inside from a previous shower. His heavy breathing lessened as he heard the noise. He stood in a batting position and just waited as his heart pounded at a rapid speed. His wife was lying in the hall unconscious. She had been knocked out with the end of the pistol by one of the intruders. They could only take the screaming so much.

The little boy was still nowhere to be found, but Ben could feel him in the room somewhere. One of the intruders was a woman. In the dream I could see her blonde hair hanging out from the back of her mask. What type of woman would be into this kind of thing? "Honey, stay behind me and walk slow. He's in here somewhere." The man says. They were a couple, maybe married. Ben grips the bat tighter sensing them getting closer, his wife still motionless in the hallway. The blonde woman whips open the closet door, and points her pistol towards the clothes, but there was no one inside. They sift through the little boy's clothes yet still find no one. Sweat started to run down the sides of Bens face, and the bat started to shake in his hand. Just the thought of his little boy being caught would devastate him. He could no longer hear his wife screaming so he didn't know if she was dead or alive, but there was only a matter of time before he was caught too. So he had to do something, and quick.

He brushed the curtains back and languidly stepped out of the tub and stood behind the door in the same batting position. His wife was consciously coming to as her fingers start to move. The two wanderers tiptoe towards the bathroom. Ben felt them breathing from behind the door as he gripped the bat as tight as he could, ready to swing at any moment. The man puts his hand on the woman's stomach and pushes her back behind him. The mannerisms they showed indicated that they cared for each other deeply. They were more than partners or killers. They were lovers. The man picks his right leg up and lunges it full force towards the door breaking the lock. Ben comes out from behind the broken door and starts to swing the bat, knocking the infiltrator in the head. The woman fires off her gun as Ben ducks behind the side of the wall in the bathroom as sheet rock powder smokes up the room. As the woman walks forward Ben's wife lets out an enormous shrill and lunges onto the blonde's back, causing her to fall onto the bathroom floor letting off more gunshots in every direction as she plummeted to the ground. Blood immediately ran through the cracks of the tile as the stream led from Ben's leg. "Sarah go! Get out of here!" He yells.

"Nick! What are you doing? Get up!" The blonde says as she turns on her back and points the gun towards Ben. As the man starts to come to, Sarah grabs his gun and points it at her. "Drop it!" Sarah yells.

"No you drop it!" The woman says. As they stood there with guns drawn and blood still rushing from Ben's leg, the man quickly knocks Sarah's feet out from under her, and as the woman's focus shifts towards the commotion, Ben instantly swings the bat knocking the pistol from her hands. Sarah picks up the gun and takes off down the hall with Ben limping behind her dodging bullets left and right. They had nowhere to go. They could only linger upstairs for the time being because the stairs they had were spiral. If they attempted to run out of the house they would be taken out immediately from the top of the staircase.

The two prowlers took off down the hall following the blood trail that led to the guest bedroom that wasn't yet furnished. Sarah darted in first, running so fast she tripped over her untied shoe laces, as the pistol slid against the corner of the wall. She attempted to crawl towards it but it was so dark in the room she couldn't see it. No light from the windows and the intruders had shut off the breakers before entering the house so it was pitch black. The lightest part of the room was by the door where the emergency, battery powered nightlight from the kid's room lit up part of the hallway. In the gloom there stood the shadows of the couple dressed in black by the foot of the door. Ben quickly picked Sarah up off the floor and stooped low against the wall. Although it was dark, they were in plain sight. Nowhere to run and nowhere to hide. With no weapon to defend them with, they stood low kneeling on the floor with their hands reached out in front of them.

"Don't shoot, please don't shoot." Sarah says.

"Where is it?" The blonde says.

"We don't have it anymore." Ben said nervously. Nick knocks Ben on the side of the head hard with the end of the pistol.

"I'm going to ask you again. Where is it?!" The woman yells. She cocks her gun and points it at Sarah.

"Lacey don't!" Nick says loudly. "If you don't tell me where the tape is I will kill you myself." He says.

"I wouldn't do that if I were you. The tape was sent to a friend, and if anything happens to us he was told to mail it to the authorities immediately." Ben says.

"What!?" Nick screams. He grabs Ben by the collar of his shirt and slams him up against the wall. As he let go, Ben falls straight back to the ground splashing into the pool of blood that had spilled out from his wound. He was weak and his face was pale. He needed medical attention immediately. Sarah hovered over him crying. "Leave him alone." She says still whimpering. She wails as Nick kicks her in the ribs and pulling her from Ben.

"You've only got one option here, and I think you both know what that option is. Now either you tell me or it's over for you." Nick says.

Ben struggles to stand up as Sarah holds onto his arm helping him to his feet. His white linen pants were soaked with blood, and his head was throbbing. His left leg where he was wounded was wobbling as he stood tall. "If we give it to you, it's already over for us. We know too much, and what you did to Sarah's parents is unforgiveable. You'll never walk away from this, even if it kills us." Ben says.

"What is it you want?!" Lacey yells. Ben started to stagger. He leans up against the wall to ease the pain in his leg, staring at Nick in the eyes as he clung tightly to Sarah.

"Justice." He says softly.

"So what do we do then huh? Should we just walk away, and act like this never happened?" Nick says.

Lacey stood there still pointing the gun towards Ben. Ben knew they weren't going to keep them alive. With fear of them relocating and potentially calling the cops, they didn't know what else to do. The only peace they had in their minds was knowing that their little boy was nowhere to be found to see this. His heart couldn't take it. He was old enough to know what was going on, and watching his parents die would traumatize him for life.

"If you leave now, you have my word…this never happened." Sarah says. Lacey grips the handle of the pistol.

"No, we can't take that chance." She says as she fires the gun at Sarah, hitting her in the chest.

"Nooooo!" Ben yells, as he pushes himself off of the wall and dives towards Lacey as they both struggle with the weapon in the air. Sarah was down, but still breathing. Nick rushes to assist his companion, grabbing Ben by the neck putting him in a chokehold dragging him away from Lacey as she fires off another shot piercing his side. Not even a second after, another shot goes off. Lacey looks at her gun in confusion. The second shot didn't come from her. All three of them look around the room, and saw nothing. Not even movement.

Lacey tilts her head with her eyes locked on Nick. She starts to stagger as blood starts to protrude from her mouth. She falls to the ground. Nick runs over to grab the gun and as soon as he does another two shots are fired taking him out before he makes a move. Lacey gasps for breathe and turns her head to the side as she sees Nick lying in a layer of blood next to her.

CHAPTER TWENTY-TWO

"Nick…Nick." In a frail voice. There was no answer. Tears roll down her face as she takes her last breathe. "Partner and lovers." She says before she lies there still, with her eyes still open. Ben lay there on the ground with his hands up. "Who are you?! Who is there?!" He screams out. He could see nothing, but could only hear the gun being dropped on the floor.

"Dad…it's me." A little voice says.

"Stephen? Oh my lord, how did you…how in God's name did you…?" He stutters in disbelief.

"I heard a loud banging so I crawled fast into this room. No one ever comes in here. Dad… are you okay? I'm scared." Stephen says as he crawls toward him. Ben hears a slight moan coming from behind him. It was Sarah. She was still alive. It took everything within her to speak.

"He's okay right?" She says. "Yea sweat heart he's okay and you're going to be okay too don't worry." Ben says.

"Honey?" She asked in a faint voice.

"Yeah babe what is it?" He replies.

"Do you love me?" She asks.

"You know I do." He says weeping.

"I thought you might." She says. Ben began to cry as he held her in his arms as she took her last breathe. Stephen scooted back over in the corner and balled himself with his head in between his knees. He's seen too much already and his brain hasn't registered it all yet. He blames himself for not firing off the gun sooner, but he was too scared to shoot, and it was way too dark to tell who it was at the time. Ben didn't question it in his mind. He knew it was a difficult thing for a ten year old to do, and didn't blame him for not reacting immediately. He was surprised he shot the gun in the first place.

"Who's up there?!" A voice called out from down stairs. To Ben it sounded like a third party of the intruders. The voice sounded familiar. Stephen sat there in the corner with his forehead still pressed against his knee. It was like déjà vu. His feet getting wet as blood ran into his socks from the middle of the room. Ben was losing too much blood. He became cold, and helpless. As the footsteps through the halls grew louder, Ben swung his arms out with all the strength he had left. "Go Stephen... Just go!" He says breathing heavily. A stream of tears ran down Stephen's face. He didn't want to leave him. He never stood up, he just sat there. Ben had no more breath left for words. A figure approaches the door and a bright light shines inside the room. Stephen sees his mother lying there in a pool of blood, and his father at her side struggling to breathe.

Stephen grabs the gun and points it towards the light squinting heavily. "What in God's name! Sherri, call 911 now! We need an ambulance quick!" The neighbors saw the door wide open and came to check on them after hearing the ruckus, only to find a blood bath in the middle of the floor of the guest bedroom. Sherri covered her mouth and started to dry heave repeatedly. The flashlight shone over Stephen. "Anyone else in here?" The man called out.

Still dreaming, I felt my heart skip a beat as I saw the little boy's teary eyes. It was me. I immediately awoke panting excessively. I nudged Venessa awake immediately.

"What? Stop it Alex, what is it?" She said in an irritable tone.

"I just had a terrible nightmare!" I said breathing as if I needed an inhaler. My shirt was soaked with sweat once again, and after a few days without showering my scent was repulsive.

"What about?" Venessa asks. "Did you have another one?! What was it about?!" She yelled. As I caught my breath I went to speak then the door swung open.

"What's going on up here?" Tyler asked, entering.

"He just had a bad dream that's all." Venessa answered.

I shook my head slightly giving her the notion that was the wrong thing to say. I saw the apology on her face.

"A bad dream huh? I wouldn't call that a bad dream at all, just truth." He said. Tan comes running in the door behind him. "What's going on?" He asked.

"It appears our dream catcher had a break through, isn't that right sport?" Tyler asked. "How many?" Tan asks. I sat there in silence disturbed by the thoughts crawling through my head. "You heard the man, how many?" Tyler asks as he stepped towards me. I take a gulp.

"Just a few." I muttered. Tyler inched closer to me. His hands behind his back made me nervous. Tan stood behind and gave me a wink. I didn't know what it meant, maybe for doing what he asked and remembering, but remembering what? All I've done is realized two people that were supposedly my parents were murdered and I defended them by turning into a killer myself.

"So what happened in those dreams?" Tyler asked.

"They were just dreams. People have them all the time, what's the big deal?!"

As soon as I got the words out, Tyler rushed towards me and drop kicks me in the stomach. As the chair flew back one of the legs brook as I took a header to the floor. Tan darted in to hold him back by wrapping his arm around his upper chest sternly as Tyler fought his restraint. Venessa struggled to break free of the rope moving wildly in the chair causing her chair to tip over as well. I lay there on the floor trying to breathe air back into my lungs as we stared each other in the eyes.

"Just a dream?! You have no idea! No idea!" Tyler yells still struggling to break free of Tan's grip. He finally calmed down, and Tan released him. He walked over to me and lifted me up by my shirt with both hands. "You're going to tell me what you saw." He said.

I tilted my head around Tyler to see Tan behind him nodding his head yes. "I...I don't remember." I say timidly.

Tan lowers his head, and puts his hand on his forehead. Tyler throws me back down on the ground with force, breaking the chair in half. My body attempted to lock down and my eye sight left the room and shot into some sort of hospital where I sat Indian style on the floor playing with Legos. I look around and see patients that are ill, scary even. All their mannerisms were strange, and I wanted to throw up every second because of the sour smell striking my nostrils. I stare at the Lego men as I stack them on top of the pyramid I spent time building and a figure walks past me, slings his foot out, and kicks my project, scattering pieces all over the floor. I look back at the kid as he keeps walking with his hands in his pockets, whistling a tune.

"Alex? Alex?!" I hear Venessa's voice as I come to. She slides towards me still attached to the chair. Tyler steps on her hand as she reaches out to grab mine. She lets out a wail leaving a dreadful grinding noise in my ear from hearing the bones crack in her little fingers. Tan stood back and bit his fingernails nervously.

"Don't play with me! The more you play these little games, the more you will get hurt." Tyler says. "Let's go man; I think they got the picture." Tan says. I spit a dark blob of blood out of my mouth, and tried to roll on my back. The pain was unbearable; I couldn't give him what he wanted. Not yet. He could kill me after I tell him for all I know.

We lay there alone, helpless in the room with our bodies aching. We heard fussing from Tyler and Tan in the next room. "So what do we do now, we know he knows and that's all that matters right?" Tan asked.

"No, it's not over yet. He may know a lot, but he doesn't know it all. I can feel it." Tyler answered.

"Cut them a break man, I think they've been through enough already."

"You don't decide anything! I determine that! If you want to help them go ahead, but we all know under your circumstances that wouldn't be a good idea."

"Listen, I don't deserve to be blackmailed anymore about that, especially after all we've been through all these years. It was an accident. I was drunk and stupid, and if I get caught that's the end of me!"

"I told you not to drive that night. I told you to wait until you sobered up, and now look what you've done! That poor family is without a wife and mother because of you, and you didn't even stop to see if she was okay. You deserve whatever is coming to you whether its blackmail or jail."

"But I…" "But nothing. Either you're onboard with this or you're not. Your choice!" Tyler yelled.

We heard a door slam. Tan walks in and stares at us lying on the floor. He picks up Venessa's chair, and slides her towards the window so she can lay her head on the wall. "I'll have to get you another chair, man. Sorry about all of this." Tan said.

"What are you going to do next? How are you going to help us?" I ask. He picks up the broken chair.

"I'm sorry. It's out of my hands." He said.

"What do you mean?"

"Look, I can't explain why but, I just can't help you. That's it." Tan couldn't even look me in the eyes. He had all the power to set us free, but gave up on us to save himself. I hated him. He was probably never going to help us in the first place. It was just a game. They're both dead to me at this point, and if one more finger is laid on Venessa, I may turn into a psycho, I thought. This was all because of me and I felt like every time she bled, that blood was on my hands.

"I'm sorry about all of this Venessa and everything I've put you through. You don't deserve any of this and somehow I'll make it right". I told her.

"We're in this together, ok? Neither one of us deserved this or could have known this was coming. Let's just stay strong, and get home. Deal?" She said.

"Deal."

CHAPTER TWENTY-THREE

Venessa stares out the window, peering at a café across the street. "Man what I would do for a ham sandwich right about now." She says. A gentleman wearing an apron walked outside the café to take a smoke break. He looked familiar to her but she couldn't place where she knew him from. He looked around, and his head stops turning. He stared right at the boarded up window, and in between that plywood he saw a pair of eyes, a pair of eyes that he had seen before. He walked closer towards the house to get a better look and just stares for the next minute while the wind took the smoke blowing out of his mouth. His eyes widen. He drops the cigarette and puts it out with his shoe, grinding it onto the street and briskly walked back into the café.

"What's going on Venessa? What are you looking at?"

"About the café across the street, have we been there before?"

"No I don't think so. What's the name of it?" I asked. She squinted to look harder. "It says café Louista." She says.

"Wait a second, café Louista?! Isn't that the name of Cole's brother's place? You know the doorman from the hotel."

"That's what it is. It's Derek!"

"What street is this, can you see the sign?"

"Yes, it's Court Street."

"That's his place. Did he look up? Did he see you?" I asked in a low voice, fearful of Tyler hearing me.

"Calm down, I don't know for sure. He peaked up here for a bit, but the he just walked back inside after he finished his cigarette." She explained.

"Oh my gosh, he's coming back out! With a cop!" she shouted excited.

"Shhhhh! What are you thinking? What if they hear you?"

"He must have known something was weird about the plywood huh? I'll put money on it. We're saved!" She said in a lower voice.

Venessa watched as Derek and the cop walked across the street to the house. The loud bang on the door was a great sign of relief. I was so glad this was over. I thought back to when I would wake up to the smell of pancakes in the morning, my brothers tossing the football back and forth to me, and even some of the bad memories came to mind, but ironically it didn't even come close to matching what Venessa and I had gone through. Downstairs we heard Tyler answer the door.

"Hello officer, how can I help you?" He asked.

"Well a citizen saw something questionable on the second floor of this house, so I'm just here to check it out and make sure everything's okay." The cop said.

"Well sure come on in. Nothing questionable here, just my parent's house, but they're out at the moment so I'm just here looking after it."

"You want me to show him around?" Tan asks.

"That would be great Tan; I have food in the oven I need to check on anyway." Tyler says. We could hear Tan walking them slowly to each room with the cop following behind him.

"Can we check the upstairs half?" Derek asked.

"Yeah let's do that." The cop says. "Just show us the way." He added.

The chances of the officer entering the bloody room with two battered teenagers were high, but he hadn't thought that far ahead. Derek knew exactly where to look however, he knew something wasn't right. My eyes were locked on the doorknob praying that the person behind that door would be wearing blue. The first time in my life I would be glad to see a cop.

"Who's wheelchair?" The officer asked. "Uh…uh it's Tyler's grandmother's. We, I mean he keeps an extra here when she comes to visit." Tan answered.

"Oh, well that's nice. So what's in these other rooms?" I heard footsteps walking towards the door. This is it. This is really happening. The doorknob started to slightly turn. Tan was so nervous I could hear him breathing through the door. There's nothing like seeing a big smile on Venessa's face, at least something to take her mind off the pain in her broken fingers.

"You know what? I'm so embarrassed this is the room I stay in, and it's really messy. I'll clean it first then we can come back. Tan starts to walk away.

"I don't mind messy." The cop said.

"Okay…suit yourself." Tan replied nervously. Tan slowly turned the knob and opened the door, poking his head in first.

"Yeah it's pretty bad in here, are you sure you wanna see it?" Tan asked.

He opened the door wider and the cop looked and saw

Venessa and I bloody, bruised, and tied up. Our mouths weren't tied with cloth anymore, and we didn't yell because if something went wrong, we were sure to be punished, and our bodies couldn't take another hit. We just stared at the officer in disbelief and as his eyes widened he quickly whipped out his gun, and pointed it at Tan.

"Don't move!" Out of nowhere he took a smack to the head with a drain pipe, and fell to the ground dropping his gun. It was Tyler. Derek strikes Tyler in the face, and he hits the floor. Tan goes behind Derek and puts him in a choker until he falls asleep. His struggling ceased and his body fell to the ground. Our mouths dropped. Tyler picked up the gun and kicked the cop's body out of the way as he entered the room.

"You think you're slick huh? Who was it?" Neither one of us said a word, just looked at him in disgust as we watched him take our freedom away. Thinking back, it's probably a good thing we didn't scream for help. It would only be another broken bone added to the equation. Tan stood there with his hand around his mouth. His eyes wide open, shocked by what he saw.

"What do we do now?" Tan asked, scared.

"Calm down you wimp. We'll take care of it just like we're gonna take care of them." A stream of tears ran down Venessa's face. My eyes were flooded, and could easily burst at any moment, but I tried to stay strong. I had to stay strong for both of us. Tyler dragged the unconscious bodies downstairs to the basement and Tan grabbed Venessa up from the chair and followed. I sat there and thought about home. What it would be like to be home again. I couldn't get it off my mind.

I heard footsteps rushing upstairs. Tyler kicked open the door, came over and grabbed me by my neck, and dragged me out of the room. The pain was unbearable. The air to breathe minimal. "Stop!" I yelled. He kept going. I grabbed the hand holding me, relieving some tension. He yanked back trying to pull me into the basement, holding both my arm and my neck. I struggled to break free, and once he let go of my arm I grabbed his shirt and yanked and he came tumbling down with me. I punched him several times in the face and chest, as many as I could and as hard as I could. We slid down the last few steps and hit the floor hard. Tyler held his back in pain. As I crawled over as quickly as I could to get more licks in, I was met with a boot to the gut. I struggle to breathe as I tried to lift my body back up off the ground. Above me Tan smiled. If I go down I go down swinging, I thought. He attempted to kick again, but I caught his foot, twisting it sideways so he fell on top of Tyler. My upper body strength was diminishing and I was still trying to catch my breath. I held my stomach as I crawled towards the drain pipe lying against the wall. I have to end this, I thought. *I'll do whatever I have to do.*

I heard Venessa calling my name from the basement. I ignored it for the time being. She would understand when it was all over. I could almost reach the pipe. More effort poured into my reach as I launched my body towards the wall. Suddenly my head started to pound. It was like a migraine but three times the pain. I put my hands on my head and rolled on my back screaming at the top of my lungs. Blood ran down from my nose as I lay there in panic and fear. I tried once more to retrieve to pipe seeing that it was my only weapon to defend myself. As my stomach lifted off the ground, Venessa's voice starts to fade out as I collapsed back onto the floor and my mind flickered back and forth from black to white. I start to convulse. I held my shirt collar in my mouth and bit down hard as my body shook. My mind flashed into a familiar room, the same hospital room. There I sat Indian style on the carpet highly aggravated as I turned around to see who scattered my Legos across the floor. The boy just kept walking, whistling a tune with his hands in his pockets. I took one of the Legos and threw it at his back. He stops. Then he slowly turns around. I can feel my body twitching more, and my eyes can't seem to open at the moment. His smirk was evil and his eyes were full of pain. It was a young Tyler. He turned his head and keeps walking.

CHAPTER TWENT-FOUR

My body relaxed and my eyelids slowly opened up. I lay limp on the floor. I looked up to see Tyler and Tan standing over me. Tyler gave the same evil smirk as he did in my vision. He hadn't changed at all. I glanced over at the pipe. It was within my reach but there was nothing I could do then. I felt lifeless. They clearly saw I couldn't struggle so they didn't even bother punishing me. Watching me convulse was enough I supposed. From what I saw, I did a pretty good number on them. I would've smiled with pride, but that would've added to the pain. It wasn't worth it. They carried me down to the basement with my feet dangling to join the others. The cop looked worse than before, and so did Derek. They must have beaten them too.

Venessa still looked battered but luckily appeared the same as the last time I saw her, thankfully. I would never forgive myself if I made her suffer even more because of my attempt at heroism. The officer was shackled up to a pole with his own handcuffs. I don't know why that almost made me laugh. I felt bad for even thinking about laughing. Venessa was also tied to a pole a couple inches away from the cop. They were almost back to back. Derek was tied to a rusty old pipe attached to the wall. That left me. They tied my arms behind my back and stuck me in the corner away from everyone else near the window. It was dark and there was a small drip coming from the ceiling above. I hung my head as they slammed the door behind them.

"Are you okay Alex?" Venessa whispered.

"Yeah I'm fine." I answered. "Just had a mild seizure. I think I'm coming into some answers though."

"Really? Like what?"

"Well my visions, dreams, or whatever they are came again, and Tyler was in it, as a kid. So far my parents die, I kill two people, and Tyler and I are in some weird mental hospital together as little boys."

"Wow, so what's your guess?" She asked.

"Well I don't have all the answers, my dreams are just filling up. The thing is they can't be memories because the people in my dreams I never met in real life."

"Tyler's in it and you know him."

"Yeah but not as a child." I said.

"So where do we go from here?"

"Well we gotta look for clues in the dreams. A lot is missing, but my body is too weak to think. He brought us here for a reason." I explained.

The cop comes to. "Rise and shine!" I said to him. "You took a crack to the head boss man. You were our only way out and you blew it."

"Leave him alone Alex" Venessa says. "It's hard enough being down here. At least he tried to help."

"Well, who's gonna run my business if I'm not there?" Derek said coming to also. I couldn't believe my ears. We were all about to die, and Derek was thinking about money. We tuned him out. I felt like we were in prison. Of course the rest of them didn't have to go through what Venessa and I did but them trying to help meant a lot. With the two new comers, there is no way they were going to let us walk, especially since there was a cop involved. There was only one thing left to do. One thing that had to be done or we were finished for good and could kiss our families goodbye. We had to break out. I was able to reach one half which was unfortunately the smallest. The cop started fidgeting around behind him.

"What are you doing?" Venessa asked annoyed by his movement.

"Those idiots took my key to the hand cuffs, but I'm checking to see if they took my extra." He says.

"Where is it?" He struggled to reach for his back pocket. "It must be in here still." He said. I was hoping it was. If there was a way we were getting out of here it was with that key. I brainstormed for some other ways, but came up with nothing. "I think I feel it." The cop said. "Yep it's in here!" He takes it out and starts to rattle the lock.

My heart jumps. "Can you get it?" Derek asked eagerly.

"Be patient man it's harder when you can't see it of course." He starts to jimmy it again, and Tan opened the door. The cop dropped the key instantly, and hid it under his butt. Tan walked near him. Everything was silent. I couldn't stand to look at his face after what he did. I thought he was going to help. Turns out whatever Tyler told him made him turn to his side for good. He found himself in too deep, and by the time he realized it; it was too late.

Venessa was nodding in and out of sleep since we got down here. She was sick, and her face had looked pale. Tan stared at the cop. "They're looking for you." He said. Tan and Tyler had stripped him of his wallet, and all of his belongings including his walkie talkie. Thankfully they missed his spare key.

"That's all you came down here to tell me? I'm a cop that hasn't answered my dispatch; of course they're looking for me." He said.

Tan shrugged. "Play nice everyone."

For some reason I hated when they left the room. Once they did we weren't sure when they were going to come back, or if they were going to come back at all. "So what's your name any way officer?" I asked. I don't like cops, but since one held the key to our freedom, I thought I'd do what Tan sarcastically suggested and play nice.

"It's Jolan." He says retrieving the key from under him. He started again at the lock. I could tell everyone was waiting for that one sound. That clicking sound that would determine our freedom. If he did get loose he could climb out the window and run and get help, I'm talking a swat team.

I wanted nothing to get in the way of stopping us. Jolan being a cop would be our best bet. The lock clicked. "Got it." Jolan says. Venessa looked at me and a single tear rolled down her face.

Derek stopped pulling on the rusty pipe. "Did you just do what I think you did?" He says. "Yes, but we can't get comfortable just yet." Jolan said and he was right. Even if we did get out of the window we would have to get away without getting caught, and Tyler had taken his belt which held his gun, taser, and pepper spray. There would probably be a good chance we could escape if they didn't see us through the window in Tyler's room, which was in plain sight of the direction we would have to go. The main thing that would slow us down is me.

My wheelchair was still upstairs, and someone would

have to carry me out. It would take some time, and as frequent as they came down to check on us, we were sure to be caught, and Jolan knew it. He stayed with his hands behind his back until we thought of a plan. I thought of a thousand ways, but I knew how it had to be. This was my mess and I had to clean it up.

"Listen, you guys have to go without me. You can't get me out without getting caught." I say.

"No! You're coming." Venessa objected.

"It's the only way, trust me. None of this involves any of you. Just go quickly and get help, I can handle it down here until then." It got quiet. I looked at Jolan for approval, and he nodded his head. Derek didn't like the plan but knew it was the only way. Venessa stared me in the eyes and more tears started to fall. "It just has to be done." I said softly.

"Well if we're going to do this we have to get a move on." Jolan says. He frees himself from the cuffs and rubs his wrist. "Never thought I'd see the day where I'd be wearing my own handcuffs." He said then quickly untied everyone, and one by one they each started towards the opening. It was windy outside and the whistling noise came in through the window.

"We have to hurry, that noise is too loud." Jolan was the last one through before he lifted the other two through the open window. He starts to close the latch. "Don't worry man, we'll be right back." He said and I gave him a wink. As the latch closed behind him a piece of paper that was lying on the ledge flew down and landed next to me. It was a picture. I picked it up, and looked fixedly at it. My heart throbbed out of my stomach as I stared at the family photo. Tyler was in the photo. It was him as a little boy, the same little boy from my dream that knocked over my Legos over. That part didn't freak me out as much. As I looked at the picture harder my head was struck with a sharp pain. My mind flashed to a memory - a beautiful living room with a large television. I sat in front of it in the middle of the floor bouncing a tennis ball watching Sponge Bob.

"Would you like some iced tea?" A voice says. I looked behind me and there she was. It was Lacey.

"Sure, thank you." I answer.

"Now I have a question for you sweetheart." "Yeah,

what's that?" I gulp the tea down, and set the glass on the coffee table.

"Do you know what this is?" She holds up a video cassette tape. "Of course! I watch movies on them all the time!" I reply.

"Does mommy and daddy have one?"

"Yeah they do, plenty! Do you need a movie because I can ask?"

"No, no, no, that's okay sweetie, I'll ask them." She takes the empty cup from the table. "Would you like some more?" She asked.

"Please?" I say politely. She walks to the kitchen and all I hear is whispering. I try to ease drop, but their voices were too faint. Then it gets a bit louder. Me being a nosey child, I stop bouncing the ball to listen in.

"He doesn't know anything, he can't help."

"Well then we just have to find another way. That tape could destroy us if it's leaked. It has our faces on it and everything!"

"Don't worry we'll find a way."

"We shouldn't have done it. It was stupid, and now

we could go to jail for the rest of our lives."

"Hush woman, I said we'll get the tape. We had to do what was best for our family, and that money will set us up for life. Look around you. Do you think we would have all this if we didn't do what we did? Now let's quick arguing about it and stay focused on what we have to do."

"Okay, partners and lovers?"

"Yes, partners and lovers."

My head turned back to the TV quickly as Lacey peaks her head around the corner. I started to bounce the ball again. "Here's your tea!" She says cheerily. She sets the drink in my hand, and

I open my eyes finding myself gripping the picture firmly.

CHAPTER TWENTY-FIVE

Lacey and Nick are his parents? So everything I've been "dreaming" was real. I figured as much before but then it all hit home. This is why he was keeping me here, and this is why I'm going through all of this. I killed his parents, and that is what he wanted me to remember. How could I forget all of this? It was like my memory had been erased. I sat there for a second and pondered some more. Every time I went without my shots these visions occurred. I knew the shots or the lack thereof was the reason, but maybe the purpose for the shots were to block out the past altogether. I sat there in a confused state as I talked to myself some more. Time had gone by and no sign of rescue. It probably just felt like a long time.

There was no clock down there either. I tried to look up towards the window, but couldn't see much. I stared at the door praying no one would enter. The moment that locked door was opened the gig was up. My heart pounded in my chest. I hadn't gotten much sleep beyond restless, vision filled dozes since I'd been there, but I felt wide awake. Too awake, to the point where I flinched at every sound. My eyes were wide open at all times; looking over my shoulder and expecting the worst. It couldn't be healthy. Is this how it's going to be when I get out of here and go back to daily life... if I get out of here, I wondered? The odds were against me, and I still heard no sign of return from the rest of the crew. Then out of nowhere I heard the sound of air being beat into submission. *Could that be a helicopter?* The noise got louder. It was a helicopter, it had to be. I still couldn't see outside, but I knew it was. Was it there for me? Did they find rescue? I wanted to get excited, but before I got my hopes up I wanted to know for sure.

The doorknob rattled. "What in the..." I heard Tyler behind the door. I quickly concealed the picture. I used every ounce of strength I had to free myself from the rope, but it wouldn't budge. My body was extremely weak, but my mind still felt sharp. Or maybe I was in a delusional state of panic and paranoia to keep myself alive. It felt useful at the moment, whatever it was. The rattling behind the door stopped briefly, and I only had a minute or two before he came back with the key. There was nothing I could do. I sat there helplessly tied up with no legs to get up, kick back, or run. The helicopter noise slowly drifted away. My heart dropped. At that moment I felt my mind release. My worry wasn't gone, but settled. This had to be the end. There was no way he was going to let me live. My heart raced as I pushed my back against the wall, as if it hid farther away from the enemy. It was more soothing in my mind to think that it did. The sound of sirens sounded in the distance. It sounded like multiple police cars arriving at the scene. I wasn't relieved yet.

My life was still in danger, and if there's one thing I'd learned through the entire ordeal was 'don't get your hopes up'. Tyler stood by the door with a kitchen knife and ran towards me.

"Get up! You guys think you're clever, you haven't seen anything yet!" He cut me loose, yanked me up by the collar of my shirt which was already torn, and head butted me back down on the floor. The pain was excruciating, but my eyes were locked on the knife and where it was headed. He was hesitant to use it. He dragged me up the stairs.

"Freeze!" a cop yells. Tyler dropped the knife and quickly took out Jolan's gun and shoots the man instantly. He gets a firm grip on my shirt and starts up the stairs again dragging me into the same room we were held captive in.

"You've had enough time. Now talk." He ordered.

"What are you talking about?" I say trying to act dumbfounded. He cocks the gun.

"I'm going to give you one last chance, and if I don't hear what I want I'm going to pull the trigger!" He pressed the muzzle against my temple.

"I killed them! I killed your parents!" I cried out. Tyler stepped back slowly. "I killed your parents; I saw it in my vision. I saw everything." I put my hands in front of my face.

The room was quiet for a minute. I heard the trampling of feet charging upstairs. Tyler slowly turned his head towards the door.

"Now you see? Now you see why this had to happen?" He asked.

"My parents are dead too because of yours, what did you expect me to do?!" I screamed. The footsteps became louder. "What did you expect me to do?"

He gripped the gun and calmly pointed it towards me. His finger leaning on the trigger; one slight move it was lights out for me. I closed my eyes and thought of my family. I thought of my brothers and Dr. Browden. Then as his finger pressed against the trigger one more person ran through my mind. I sluggishly reached up to feel my chest as the blood ran out. My eyes blurred as I opened them, and right before I closed them one last time an army of figures came in. I couldn't see well, but saw Tyler shift towards the door with the gun. The noise of firearms sounded from every direction. Then my eyes closed.

My life never really flashed before my eyes. Not until now. I mean of course we think about our family and what happens if one day we tragically die, but this was like no dream I could ever envision. There was no white light like everyone says there is. There was just my family. They were all outside in the front yard playing catch with the football, even my mother. She was usually cooking around that time of day. They were laughing and carrying on. It looked like so much fun and I wanted to be there so badly. I felt my heart beat slower and slower as I pictured them. Then there I go, rolling out of the house with my hands up with an enormous smile on my face.

"Here, throw it over here!" I said. My brother leans back and lobs it towards me. As I catch it my mother runs towards me to with the fake tackle. This is life. This is what I can't lose, not family. It's all I've got. I couldn't be the missing piece to that beautiful puzzle that was my folks. My eyes barely opened. I tried to move, but I just fell onto my stomach. Blood was still drooling from my mouth as I press against my chest to try to stop the bleeding. The pain was unbearable, but it was my only option for the time being. I heard footsteps coming. For once I felt like I could breathe. I hate to say it but, seeing Tyler lying breathless on the floor was my only escape from paranoia. It was finally gone. I looked up as the person entered the room, it was Cole. Not the person I expected to see at the time.

"Don't move," He said, "Help is on the way." The sirens from outside made my head throb even more, my awareness shutting on and off. The medics rushed up the stairs with a stretcher, and hooked me up to an oxygen tube as Cole held my hand. As I was carried outside I looked around. I looked around in every direction, but all I saw was Tan sitting in the cop car.

"Don't worry," Cole says, "They're all safe. They're getting treated right now."

I stopped searching. My heart beat is was still slow. I fought to stay awake the entire ride to the hospital, but not sure if I'd make it that far. When we did make it I was surprised. I just wanted to see my family one last time if it was going to end there. I hated thinking like that but the way I felt left me no other choice. Optimism was no longer my strong suit.

Later I lay there in the hospital bed, and Venessa rushed through the door to collapse at my bedside. She didn't say anything but just knelt there holding my hand. I saw Cole sitting in the chair across from me with his head down.

"I called our parents Alex. They're on their way.

They were already on the flight when I called and they should land shortly." Venessa said. She gripped my hand tighter. A smile came over my face. "I just...I just need to rest." I said softly.

Resting or not, I still heard the life monitoring system beeping. That's how I could tell I was still alive - that and the death grip Venessa had on my hand. It felt good though, and I was hoping in my mind she wouldn't let it go. Ever.

When I woke, my family was surrounding me. It was the best thing I could wake up to. Dr. Browden also made it. My eyes began to water making everything around me blurry. I could tell Dad was trying his best to hold back his tears, but caved as soon as Mom started to ball. Taylor and Mason sat slouched on the couch staring off into space like zombies. They weren't excepting it. The tears that filled my eyes finally fell on the sides of my pale face.

The doctor came in and talked to my parents and Dr. Browden. There were no smiles, or tears of joy as they conversed which made me nervous. Mom glanced over my way. My eyes were barely open. I stared up at the ceiling as my parents came over to hold each of my hands silently. The energy was leaving me. When I used to go to my brothers games and watch them play I sat right by the fence as close as to the field as possible imaging myself out there with them, leading the team to victory. Their legs would move so fast. They would cut to the right, and then cut to the left. I got most excited when the game was at its peak, like most people. Taylor would be running down the field with the ball being chased by the opponent, I'd swing my arms as if I was running in place, only imaging I was blocking for him. I was living a dream this whole time. As I lay on what I had come to think of as my death bed, I came to the realization that my entire life of memories as a small child had never happened. My family knew it all along and never said anything.

I start to think about the dreams I had back at Tyler's house, the visions of my parents dying, and the state I was in as a child in the mental hospital. I couldn't fault them for what they did. Forget the fact that I don't know who I really am, they saved my life. They took me in and restored me mentally. It was all so clear now. Though all this time I was still trapping myself in a make-believe world; only wishing to be like everyone else. I wanted to go back and change it. All of a sudden Todd swung open the door panting as if he had just run a mile. The nurse guarded the door not letting him in. "It's okay." I said weakly. Todd walks towards me. He was in between a cry and a smile; his face couldn't make up its mind.

"Buddy... how you hanging in there guy?" He asked calmly. His lips began to quiver and he shut them tight so they would stop. More tears fell on the sides of my face.

"Hey sweetheart, you're gonna make it. You just have to. None of this works without you." Venessa says weeping. I couldn't say much, but I took all the breathe I had to tell her how I really felt. In front of everyone. I signaled her to come closer with my finger. "You know, when I got shot... my life flashed before my eyes. I thought of my family, Dr. Browden..." I began to cough in the middle of my sentence.

"Shhh you don't have to talk right now." She says.

"No...let me get this out" I said. "But do you know who I thought of before my eyes closed?

The very last face I saw go through my mind...was you. I love you Venessa, and I knew it the..." she interrupts me with a kiss. The rest of the family just watched in awe, but in silence. The nurse came over to my bedside and checked my heart rate. It was slowing down. I read her name tag.

"Jamie, am I going to die?" I asked. She looked straight into my eyes.

"You know, I was once lying exactly where you are at one time, thinking the exact same thing. Look at me now." She smiled and stroked my forehead. "Who knows, maybe we are just alike." She said trying hard to smile cheerfully. I guessed, despite my love, and in spite of theirs, especially the hard won love of Venessa, it wasn't going to end well. But I liked to hear some optimism since I had none left. I glanced over at the monitor. The beeping was still there, but the gaps between them were getting longer.

"We're going to run some more test, and I'll be back

with the results shortly." The doctor said, leaving. Venessa leans in, seeing me slipping, and in what seemed to be the last move of a desperate person, pressed her lips, wet from tears, against mine hungrily. Whereas the life force had seemed before to be slipping away; a stream of affection, admiration and love for who I was - who I had become since being that scared little orphaned boy - poured through her kiss. If death wanted me after that it would have one heck of a fight.

The clipboard was sitting at the foot of my bed and Nurse Jamie accidentally swiped my foot on her reach to grab it. "Ouch!" I yell reacting to the pain. Every eye in the room went to my formerly useless legs as they twitched in response to the new sensations coursing through them. Taylor stands up from the couch as my foot jerked again.

"Wait…what? You can move your legs?"

END